GOOD HARBOR BAY

GOOD HARBOR BAY

a novel
by Barry Marsh

To Marlo

Barry Marsh

CROFTON CREEK PRESS
SOUTH BOARDMAN, MICHIGAN

First Edition
10 9 8 7 6 5 4 3 2 1

Published by Crofton Creek Press
2303 Gregg Road SW
South Boardman, Michigan 49680
E-mail: publisher@croftoncreek.com
Web site: www.croftoncreek.com

Cover design and illustrations by Jenifer Thomas

Manufactured by Thomson-Shore, Dexter, MI (USA); 562TB794, September 2009

Library of Congress Cataloging-in-Publication Data

Marsh, Barry.
    Good Harbor Bay / by Barry Marsh.
        p. cm.
    Summary: When Josh's mother is killed in a car accident, his father quits
his high-powered job in the city and they move into a northern Michigan log
cabin with his ancient and eccentric grandfather.
        ISBN 0-9767268-1-5 (978-0-9767268-1-4 : alk. paper)
    [1. Fathers and sons--Fiction. 2. Grandfathers--Fiction. 3. Country life-
-Michigan--Fiction. 4. Michigan--Fiction.] I. Title.

    PZ7.M35165Go 2009
    [Fic]--dc22

                                                        2009024734

Contents

Acknowledgments

My thanks to the many people who contributed to the creation and publication of this book. Heartfelt gratitude for the loving support of my family. Thanks also to my first young reader of the manuscript, twelve-year-old Clay Darling, and to the upper elementary class at The Children's House, An Independent Montessori School, and teachers Catherine Turnbull and Patty Anton for valuable feedback. I'm grateful to my dear friend Rose Hollander for her sincere and never-ending support and to Art DeLaurier Jr., Grace Truax, and Roberta Williams for their invaluable editorial suggestions. I'm indebted to psychologist Thomas Borgeld, PhD, for his insights into grief and loss. Thanks to Tom Cyr, owner of Black Horse LLC, for his demonstrations of logging with draft horses. Thanks also to Jackie Morrison and Mary Bush at The Business Helper. Special thanks to Doug Truax, my editor and friend, and illustrator Jenny Thomas for helping bring my ideas and words to life.

1
THE MOVE NORTH

Joshua's father called up to the loft. "Josh, breakfast is on the table. Come on, get up now. Last call."

Josh only half-heard his father. He mostly heard the wind whistling through the pines outside. An irresistible urge to nestle deeper into his puffy feather-tick mattress overwhelmed him when he heard the sandy sound of snow blowing horizontally against the windowpane above his head. The makings of another major snowstorm, he thought.

What he did not hear was the front door of the cabin opening as Grandpa Oggy entered armed with a freshly packed snowball that he lobbed into the loft, splattering Josh in the face.

Annoyed, Josh rolled onto his belly and pulled the covers over his head. "That crazy old man is at it again," he whispered to himself. From under the covers he heard the front door open, which meant that Grandpa was headed out for another snowball.

Josh poked his head out from beneath the covers. "Okay. Okay. I'm awake!" He cleared his morning throat with a slight cough. "No more snow. I'm awake, just give me a minute." He hated today and yesterday as much as the day he and his father had moved to Grandpa Oggy's cabin two months before. Josh had said he wouldn't move, but here he was. Stuck in the boonies.

Josh rubbed sleep out of his eyes and lay for a moment listening to the ticking of his alarm clock. Another day in the sticks shoveling snow and horse poop, and home-schooling in the afternoon, he thought to himself. It felt like he had been delivered to another planet, not just another part of the state.

He remembered the drive north vividly. He remembered streetlights disappearing, the time between seeing car headlights getting longer until there were none. Every so often he saw the eyes of deer and other mysterious animals glowing in the headlight beams at the edge of the forest. Sometimes the eyes seemed unattached to a body, like seeing the sudden glow of a firefly in the black of night.

Before his father turned onto Grandpa Oggy's two-track, Josh had been spooked at the sight of a coyote

running across the road. He felt like a stranger traveling through dark, unfamiliar territory. The car's headlights illuminated the tall, thick pines looming beside Grandpa's road—a green tunnel that ended at Grandpa's log cabin. And there on the front porch, with his hands in his pockets, his long white beard shining in the headlights, was Grandpa.

He couldn't forgive his father for moving him here. He didn't like anything about this isolated place he was supposed to call home. Downstate he was unhappy after he lost his mother, but this just made things worse. Much worse.

"Josh, this is the last time I'm gonna call you," his father, Noah, hollered over the clinking of iron frying pans. "Breakfast is on the table."

"I'm up. I'm up," Josh replied in an annoyed tone. To avoid more snowballs he sat on the edge of the bed and thumped his feet on the floor so his father and grandfather could hear he was getting up. He finally stood and shuffled his way over to the rail and leaned over it. He looked down and saw Peach, Grandpa Oggy's orange-and-white Brittany spaniel, curled up in her bed next to the warm wood stove. Peach was the only thing inside the cabin that could bring a smile to his face. "I'm on my way down, Peach," he said as he swung a leg onto the wooden ladder.

His dad was flipping pancakes. Josh couldn't get used to his father's longer hair, denim carpenter jeans, flannel shirt, and high-cut leather boots. He had gone totally native. Josh still expected him to be dressed in business suits and wear his hair short. Noah now worked from the cabin through the Internet or telephone, so he was always home unless he was running errands in town.

Josh watched Grandpa Oggy set the kitchen table with the usual newspaper place mats and mismatched dishes.

"Good morning, Josh," his father said.

"G'mornin', " Josh muttered. In truth, he had not felt a good morning for a long time.

"Morning, Cubby," said Grandpa Oggy.

Josh gritted his teeth. He hated the nickname "Cubby." Grandpa Oggy always had a nickname for everyone. He even called Josh's father "Smokey" for some odd reason.

Josh remembered being grossed out when he first moved to the cabin and would accidentally brush up against his grandfather's skin. It was filthy and he smelled like his stinky barn. There had been some slight improvement in Grandpa's appearance lately though. Since they'd arrived, his dad had taken it upon himself to clean Grandpa Oggy. Grandpa raised an awful fuss as he was marched to the bathroom and stripped of his overalls. Josh instinctively turned his back on them. He didn't want to watch. Josh's father had told him that when grandma was alive she would have to run the bath water when Grandpa ripened to a funk, letting him soak for a while to loosen up the dirt, and then scrub him with a horse brush. And that's just what Noah had done.

Josh climbed down the ladder and petted Peach before he sat down to breakfast.

There was one plate each for Josh and his father, and one big bowl for Grandpa. Josh watched as Grandpa put his pancakes and bacon in the bowl, chopped it all up, and poured maple syrup over the mix. Then he started eating with the big spoon he always held sideways. Breakfast, lunch, or dinner, it all got cut up in his large bowl and scooped up with his big spoon.

Even though Grandpa Oggy was old, Josh knew he was a very tough man—tall and powerfully built from a lifetime of work outdoors. His large, thick fingers were crooked from not going to a hospital after getting them pinched and broken when they were caught between logs. The left index finger was a short stub. It had been sawed off by a log-cutting blade in his sawmill years ago. Grandma had stitched up what was left of the stub with her sewing needle and thread to stop the bleeding. Grandpa Oggy proudly kept the top part of his finger in an old jelly jar on a shelf in the barn like it was a trophy. It was brown and shrunken and really ugly.

At breakfast Noah said, "So how do you guys want to handle it today? I'll plow the snow out of the barn-yard and two-track down to the main road this morning. Then I have to sit myself down to do some consulting work. It's going to take awhile. I'm planning to make a trip into Traverse City this afternoon to pick up feed and do some grocery shopping. By then the main roads should be plowed."

As soon as the first snows had come, his dad had traded in the Mercedes for a new Chevy pickup truck with a snowplow connected to the front. He said he wasn't about to hook up the plow Grandpa used behind the horses.

"I'll feed and tend to the horses," said Grandpa Oggy.

"How about you, Josh?" his father asked.

"Like I got a choice," Josh muttered. "I'll shovel horse crap and snow."

"Good," his dad said, "and after that you can come in and study."

Josh sat in silence, eating his breakfast and wondering what Trevor and his friends were doing back home. He wanted to be with them. He wanted his mother back. He wanted his old life back.

2
THE OLD LIFE

Before he was forced to move to the north country of Michigan, Josh lived downstate in Birmingham, a wealthy suburb of Detroit where his family had relocated after moving from Chicago.

Allison Ogden, Josh's mother, had quit her full-time job teaching music after the move to Birmingham. She was now a full-time mom, with the exception of tutoring music students after school. They had been in Michigan for about a year. His father, Noah Ogden, was busy with his new job. Josh was settled in and adjusting to a new home. Josh would get up and go to school. His father would get up and go to work. The household responsibilities fell to Josh's mom. Josh had gotten used to her saying that she was "running a hotel and you and your father are the guests."

Her life was all about serving others—especially Josh and his father.

And then one day after Josh's father had come home from work, after they had sat down to dinner, his father spoke up to say he had accepted a huge promotion—in New York.

His mother dropped her fork in disbelief. "Another promotion?" she said. And then again loudly, "Another promotion!" as she took her cloth napkin off of her lap, dropped it on the table, and stood. His mother very seldom lost her temper but was on a roll now.

Josh looked at his mom with wide eyes when she threw up her hands in anger. His father's head bowed down to the table. "Uh-oh, here we go," Josh said under his breath.

"Why didn't you consult me first? We're just getting settled after moving from Chicago!" his mom continued.

"Honey, this promotion is going to take us to the top of the corporate ladder. I never dreamed it would be so early in my career."

"And what about my music students? They depend on me," Allison countered.

"It was now or never, honey," his father said. "If I don't take this promotion, I'll be skipped over the next time, missing out on the stock options that would make us wealthy, very wealthy." The good news, he explained, was that with the promotion he would be at corporate headquarters, and they would never be transferred again. Josh and his mother would join him in New York within a year.

Before Josh knew it, his father was living in New York and flying home on weekends, unless he was flying to London or Japan.

3
SWEET DREAMS

The idea of the transfer hadn't bothered Josh much. Sure, he would have to make new friends, but he had learned to accept the stress on his social and school life after moving from Chicago to Birmingham. New York would just be the next challenge.

They had always lived in the suburbs. The house got bigger and fancier when they moved to Birmingham. The private country clubs were about the same in both cities, as were the private schools. Would New York be the same? He didn't know. Maybe it would be better. Either way, there was little he could do about it. As always, he would have to readjust and go with the flow. He had no other choice.

On one of the first weekends on the new job, Josh's father elected to stay in New York to get situated in his Manhattan apartment. Allison was teaching a student in the music room when Josh came home from school. He heard a violin playing Bach's Minuet No. 2 as he opened the front door and promptly escaped to his room.

Joshua settled in with his PlayStation 3 and called his best friend, Trevor, on the telephone. He had the speakerphone set to high volume so he could hear him over the music on his stereo, which he had turned up to drown out the violin music below. Trevor had found a "pretty cool" chatroom he wanted Josh to log on to. The two of them joined into the discussion at the chatroom for half an hour before Josh heard his mother at the bedroom door.

"Joshua!" his mother was shouting as she knocked on the door, which was vibrating in time to the music's booming bass.

"What?" he shouted back.

She opened the door. "How can you relax with all this noise? Come on downstairs. I'm done teaching and I want to show you something."

"Now?" Josh asked while turning down the volume on the stereo with his remote.

"Yes, I want to show you something."

Josh shrugged his shoulders, "I'm gonna have to catch you on the rebound," he said to Trevor over the speakerphone. "My mom wants me." He then punched the off button and turned to his mother at the door.

"What's up Mom?"

"I don't know. You're up here alone and I'm downstairs alone. I thought we'd just do something together. I think you'll like it."

By the time he got downstairs, his mother was sitting on the couch with the gas fireplace set on a low glow.

"Sit next to me. I think this is something you've never seen—some old pictures of when your Dad and I were in college."

"Can I get a Coke?"

"Of course. Would you get me a bottled water, please?"

As they sipped their drinks, she began to page through the album. Josh stopped her at a photograph.

"Wow," Josh said, stopping her at a somewhat yellowed color photograph. "Look at Dad's hair. It's longer than mine. It's as long as yours."

"We were only nineteen when this picture was taken," his mother chuckled. "Here's one taken when we met on the beach at Good Harbor Bay," she said softly. "That's when I was attending summer music camp at Interlochen Center for the Arts."

"By Grandpa's place?"

"Yep. We met at a bonfire party on the beach one night," she answered, again with a bit of a laugh.

"What's so funny?"

"Oh, your father was embarrassed because he thought he smelled like fish. He was working on a commercial fishing boat out of Leland Harbor that summer, and he swore he could never scrub the smell of fish off his body no matter how much soap he used."

"A fishing boat? He never told me he did that."

"Oh, he'd probably get around to it someday."

She began to describe the night of the bonfire to Josh. It seemed to give her comfort. "Back then on a pitch-black night the constellations were glistening. The shooting stars were trailing everywhere. Your father and I said that the gods had seized the evening just for us, presenting us with some sort of celestial reckoning. I can still remember your dad's face glowing on the opposite side of the campfire. I read once that falling in love at such a young, tender age is a kind of pure love that has nothing to do with careers or money."

"What's a celestial reckoning?" Josh asked.

"It's just the term your father and I created to remember that night. That's all."

He was used to her talking like this. She always had a musical way of looking at things. Listening to her was like someone describing a dream. Or like reading poetry. He didn't understand half of what she was talking about, but her words somehow comforted him.

"Let's get back to the fishing," Josh said.

"Well, your Dad reeled in nets on a fishing boat."

"What kind of fish?"

"I think it was mostly lake trout and whitefish, and then the people he worked for on the boat would sell the fish to grocery stores."

"Wow, that's a different sort of job."

"He had a different life from what you're used to. Fishing is hard work. And dangerous out there in the open water and high waves. It's what he grew up with."

They kept turning the pages of photographs. Josh noticed the similarities in his mom and dad's looks. Standing together they actually looked like brother and sister. Her medium-length hair was a dirty blond color like his dad's, their eyes the same hazel green. They both carried a smattering of freckles across their noses. Not that different from the way he looked now, he thought.

"Back then you guys looked like a couple of hippies."

His mother laughed. "We did look like hippies, but our generation came later than the real hippie generation. Don't tell your dad I told you this. This is our secret. He used to wear his hair back in a ponytail to keep his hair out of his eyes when he was working the fishing boats."

"Whoa, Dad had a ponytail?" Josh said. "Cool."

"Just remember. That's our secret. Look at these pictures of our wedding day."

Josh pointed out a picture of Grandpa and Grandma Ogden. "Look at Grandpa Ogden's hair. It's just as white and wild and bushy as it is now."

"Yeah, Grandpa Ogden kind of sticks out of the crowd more than Grandpa and Grandma Baird. Or to put it better, he doesn't care or really even know how he looks to others. I guess you could say Grandpa Ogden looks a little rough around the edges. But looks don't explain anything about your grandpa. When you get to know him, you find out he's a sweet man."

Josh didn't know Grandpa and Grandma Ogden well. He talked to them over the telephone much the same as he did with his father now that he was in New York. Josh's mother was born and raised in Chicago, where his Grandpa and Grandma Baird lived. When he and his parents lived in Chicago, he would visit the Bairds often, sometimes staying overnight with them. He visited Grandpa and Grandma Ogden only about once a year, usually during the winter school break, when he could spend the day snowboarding on the bigger slopes up north. They never stayed overnight with Grandpa and Grandma Ogden. Instead, they stayed at the same motel every year, one that had an indoor swimming pool.

"Grandpa and Grandma Ogden look kind of worn out compared to Grandpa and Grandma Baird," Josh said.

"They had different lives. My folks are city people. Grandpa and Grandma Ogden lived up north in the woods their whole life. Grandpa Ogden made a living outdoors logging trees in the forest. Before Grandma Ogden died, she helped with the logging whenever she was needed. I guess you might say they had a weathered look."

That's Mom, he thought, always putting a positive spin on things.

The last time Josh had seen Grandpa Ogden was the past fall, when his Grandma Ogden had passed away. It was the first funeral he had ever been to. It had been a strange experience and he had felt sorry for his father, who was so unhappy. The ordeal of the funeral had not affected Josh the way it did his father and grandfather. He remembered sleeping overnight at the motel and leaving the next morning because he had school the following day. The mood in the car had been very somber as they drove home.

His mother pointed to wedding ceremony pictures. "This is the very spot we met and the very spot we got married—on the beach at Good Harbor Bay."

Josh noticed a photograph of his mother wearing a crown of flowers on her head. "That's the prettiest I've ever seen you, Mom."

She closed the album.

"I had . . . we have," she said, pausing for a second, "we still have dreams of living around Good Harbor Bay when your father thinks we're financially set. We'll get there. You should never forget your dreams."

4
A COMFORTABLE LIFE

Josh was comfortable in his busy life. They had a big house with an in-ground pool in the backyard and he had a big bedroom with its own walk-in closet. He loved to show off all this to his friends when they came to visit, and his friends did the same when he went to their houses. It was an unconscious sort of social pecking order.

Josh was in deep concentration, studying in his bedroom after dinner. His father was insistent that he make the honor roll every semester, just as his father said he had done when he was in school.

His cell phone rang and he flipped it open.

"Josh," his mother said from outside his bedroom door, "no phone calls during homework."

"Okay Mom." And then he whispered quickly to his

friend, "Can't talk now; you know the move," and flipped his cell off.

His mother cracked the door open. "Turn your cell phone off until you're done studying. You have plenty of time for that later."

"It's off."

She shut the door without saying anything else.

He turned his cell back on and switched it to "vibrate." Almost immediately it vibrated with a text message. It was Trevor again. He knew it was from Trevor because they had developed their own special code. When Josh first moved to Birmingham, he had been the object of some cyberbullying. Mostly he ignored it, though it bugged him and gradually it stopped. Mysteriously the unsigned messages had started to appear again. Trevor offered to help and downloaded Josh's phantom text messages onto his laptop. Trevor had just finished "backdooring" them, and now wrote in code that he had found the hacks.

"the ansa is a posse of barbez nt gys. bcnu b4 a.m.learnin farm 2 fill u in. cya, gtta g pir," the message read.

"10-4," Josh punched in.

School was easy for Josh. He fluctuated between all A's or a mix of A's and B's, depending on what was going on socially. When he slipped down a notch in his grades, his father would come down on him like it was the end of the world. Josh knew when it was time to crank out some

grades. To calm his father, he always studied especially hard during the last marking period so he could enjoy a leisurely summer without his father being on his back. He had failed to do this two years before and spent most of the summer hearing daily lectures about all the money his father was spending on private school and the "dire consequences for your career" if Josh's grades prevented him from getting into a top college.

Josh did not take the threats too seriously, although he loved to please his father. His main concern was to put his parents enough at ease so he could have fun with his friends snowboarding in the winter and golfing and swimming at the club in the summer.

Later, when he finished with his homework, he searched his closet for the clothes he would wear to school tomorrow, making sure that what he selected had just the right labels, like Abercrombie & Fitch, Aero, or Hollister. He spotted a Burton snowboard hoodie that he wore to the slopes on weekends and to school in the winter, but the weather was getting warm, so he hung it in the rear of his closet. He could wear it next winter if it had not gone out of style by then. He liked the layered look, finishing with a thin hoodie, which was okay with the teachers as long as you didn't have the hood up over your head when entering school. Then all these layers of expensive clothing had to be taken off and put in a locker before entering class. Once in the classroom it was strictly shirt and tie.

He was excited because his father was returning from New York on the weekend and this was Josh's last week of school. Then summer vacation. And he was going to spend his first summer vacation weekend with his dad!

His father came home for the weekend on Friday evening. The next day, Saturday, Josh woke and bounded down the stairs to see him. His mother was putting the breakfast dishes in the dishwasher.

"Where's Dad?" Josh asked.

"He's at the club, golfing. He said it was an important business golf outing. He said not to worry—he'll be back in the early afternoon."

Josh was disappointed but waited for his father, who didn't return until four and then took a nap.

On Sunday Josh played golf with his mother and father,

and on Monday his father was off to Japan for two weeks. The good news was that he would fly directly back home from Japan to spend a week's vacation with them. Josh could hardly wait.

5
A GOOD PLAN

It was a beautiful sunny morning as his mother maneuvered their black BMW through the maze of rush-hour traffic on Telegraph Road, trying not to be late for Josh's first summer junior golf tournament.

"Josh," his mother said loudly. He had his earphones on, listening to music while fidgeting with the buttons on his iPod. After another try she gave up and tapped his shoulder, signaling him to remove his earphones. He thought this was a music bust to see if he was listening to music she did not allow him to listen to, so he switched the mode as he removed the earphones.

"What?" he said.

"Have you thought about what kind of sport or extra-curricular activity you'd like to get into when you start high school? You should do something. It's good for your school résumé for college."

"I guess so."

He turned off his iPod and looked at her. He did not finish answering her question right away. Last year he had gone out for a youth football team. All he remembered were the workouts—hot and sweaty and exhausting and miserable. He remembered one day in the second week of practice running around the track with full equipment on and suffering from thirst in the heat. While he ran around in circles, he looked over at the girls' and boys' high school tennis team fall practice. All they seemed to be doing was standing around talking and drinking Gatorade and ice water. He had wanted to quit, but in another day or two they were going to start full-contact scrimmages and he was eager to try this out. Maybe in high school he would be a football hero? He dreamed of catching the pass that would win the game and hearing the crowd cheer as he ran off the field.

In the first hour of contact scrimmages he got slammed to the ground. All he remembered was the world spinning and a bunch of players standing around him in a circle as he lay on his back.

"Josh, are you all right, Josh? Josh, you okay?"

"Yeah, I'm okay. That was nothin'." The rest of the afternoon he ran for his life trying not to get his head busted while being tackled. That afternoon he quit.

"Hello . . . Mother calling Josh. Mother to Josh. Are you there? Come in, please," his mother said, bringing him out of his daydream.

"I'm answering, I'm answering. I just had to gather my thoughts." He pushed the electric button that sent his window up because he wanted it quieter. His mother closed the sunroof and turned up the air conditioner. "I like sports that are more individual. Like swimming and golf. You're still playing for the team, but you have to perform more on your own. You know what I'm trying to say?"

"I wish you'd been interested in music, but I know your father thinks it's a waste of time."

"It is unless you're going to make a living at it."

"Spoken just like your father. There's more to it than that. But that's water over the dam now."

"Anyhow, swimming workouts are hard but I like them. And I'm as good at swimming as I am at golf. Golf's different though. You have to think a lot, but I like that too. At least in those sports you're not all sweaty and suffering. I hated football. I'm not into that football hero crap."

"I don't like that word. Think of another, Josh."

"Okay, stuff."

"That's not perfect, but better."

"Football's so hardcore. When I see those football guys they always seem to be limping or got some kind of hurt. Do you know what I mean?"

"That's okay by me. I didn't and don't like you to play football either. I don't want you to get hurt."

"Dad says golf's the sport. And it'll carry on into business when I grow up. A sport you can play until you're old, like dad."

"Old like dad? Do you think we're old?"

"Well, yeah. So I guess I'll do both of those sports. And the swimming is making me strong. I can tell, and so can Dad. "

His mother smiled. "That sounds like a good plan."

Lester Cobb was on his way home from the plant where he worked on the assembly line. He liked the midnight shift and always stopped for a few drinks on his way home in the morning. This morning he had gotten off early with pay because of some breakdown on the line. But Lester was angry. He'd had a run-in with the bartender at his favorite bar.

"You've had enough, Lester. You're cut off. Come on now, it's time for you to go home." The bartender had escorted him to the door and opened it. "I don't want any trouble with you, Lester."

Lester had turned to shout back some words but the door had closed, leaving him squinting in the bright morning sun.

As he drove his pickup, Lester stewed over the incident and mumbled to himself, repeating the words he had yelled at the bartender before he got kicked out: "I'm a regular in

this place! I put good money down on this bar every morn-
ing. It's guys like me that make you your livin'. I'll never step
foot in this place again."

He stopped at a party store, picked up a twelve-pack of
beer, popped one open, put it between his legs, and dropped
the rest on the passenger floor. He started his truck and was
on the road for home. He told himself he would go easy and
lay off the whiskey he had been drinking in the bar and just
drink the beer.

He had a routine. He would finish off the rest of the beers
and get at least four hours of sleep before heading back to
the plant for another shift. He swigged down the rest of
the beer he had opened five minutes ago, stuffed the empty
under his seat, and leaned his wobbling head down toward
the passenger floor to reach for another beer.

Josh returned his mom's smile. They both were pleased
with his decision as they approached the intersection on
the green light.

"What do you want for dinner tonight?" his mother
asked.

Josh was thinking pizza and turned his head to hers
and said, "I think I want . . . "

. . . with a beer in his right hand, Lester looked up from
under the console and saw black in the windshield . . .

. . . and then Josh heard an explosion of metal and glass and felt the heavy impact that slammed him and his mother against the passenger door. It happened all too quickly to even see the flying glass and steel. Glass everywhere. The blare of a car horn pierced his ears . . . nothing would stop it . . . nothing would turn it off, and he felt stinging hot liquid on his skin coming from the hissing, mangled radiator of a truck, which had struck them on the driver's side—the radiator now just two feet away from Josh's body. The truck was inside their car.

Josh felt his mother's weight and saw her lying motionless across his body. Josh began to murmur. He could get out whispers of air but no words. No words would come. Then nothing, only blackness. When he regained consciousness he was wrapped in a thermal blanket and being comforted by a police officer who was lying across the hood of the car with his head sticking through where there once was a windshield, only inches away from Josh. He heard the policeman say, "You're going to be okay. We're gonna get you out." He saw rescue workers prying open the passenger door. The police officer pulled the thermal blanket over Josh's face, momentarily blocking his vision as he felt his mother's weight leave his body. He heard the sound of bending metal and more sirens, more sirens as he lapsed back into unconsciousness.

Josh now was in his hospital bed. He had suffered a cracked clavicle in his right shoulder, a mild concussion, and some burns on his left arm. His father sat next to him.

The physicians had told Josh he was going to be fine, but his face was blank and expressionless, still reacting to what his father had just told him.

His mother was dead.

Josh was numb—stunned that in an instant she was gone. Too horrified to even feel emotion.

The police had come to the hospital to meet with Josh and his father, who had returned immediately from Japan. The police said Lester Cobb was being held in the county jail and would be charged with vehicular homicide, felony third-offense drunk driving, and would surely do a stiff prison sentence. Josh said nothing.

A few days later Josh was released from the hospital and returned home with his father. The soul-wrenching grief and hysterical bawling was over for the most part— reduced now to on-again off-again tears that came with no warning. But the mourning had only begun. Josh and his father had to gather their wits to face the funeral.

6
THE LONG TRIP NORTH

Standing next to his father, Josh saw his mother for the last time. Family and close friends congregated inside a Birmingham funeral home to say goodbye.

An Episcopalian minister recited over his mother's body as those drawn together shared their silent grief. When the service concluded, people tried to comfort Josh with words and hugs, but he found it hard to respond. He had no answer to what had happened, only heartbreak and doubt and questions.

His parents and teachers had taught him how wonderful life can be if you always try to do what is right. He had done everything according to the rules. It was not fair and he felt cheated. He was angry with the man who had stolen his mother from him. Now his life was reduced to just his father and him, and he clung to his father's side as if they were attached.

His mother was cremated and her ashes shared with Grandpa and Grandma Baird. The next day Josh and his father were on the road to Good Harbor Bay to spread her ashes on the beach. It had been no secret that Josh's mother wanted to move there someday—so now they were taking her where she had dreamed of living.

"How's your arm burn?" his father asked, trying to start a conversation.

Josh looked through the windshield in silence.

The burned left arm always itched under the bandages, but the pain had subsided and he had full use of it again. He began to move his left arm so he could rub the outside of the bandages with his right hand. His right arm was in a sling from the cracked clavicle in his shoulder, but he could take it out of the sling to stretch his arm, even though it hurt to do so.

"It still hurts a little, but it mostly itches," he said.

The only things that were undamaged and salvageable from the accident were his cell phone and the iPod he always carried in the car on long trips. But electronic gadgets hadn't entered his mind since the accident. He continued to stare in silence as the flashbacks of the past few days came and went—the accident, learning of his mother's death, the funeral—all spinning through his mind like an unstoppable horror movie.

He thought back to fiction books he had read about kids his age. He remembered dramas and tragedies, but they were just words and scenes he could simply put away when he closed the book; the strong emotions and feelings that he had experienced while reading would go away. He wished this were only a made-up story he could set aside. He could not. The scenes and sensations kept pouring back into his mind—his mother surrounded by flowers, the gentle fragrance of the flowers as the minister bid a last farewell, his father squeezing his hand tightly as they both sobbed.

He kept a secret to himself. As they were to leave the room for the last time where his mother lay, his imagination tricked him—tricked him into believing that his mother moved in her casket, that she was still alive. He realized it was just a last hope to quash the weight of reality coming down hard on him.

Josh felt imprisoned by the flashbacks as they came and went twenty-four hours a day. Torment in the waking hours, nightmares in his sleep. When he cried in the daytime, his father was there to hold him. When he cried in his sleep, his father was there to hold him. His father did most of the talking when he thought there was something important to say. It was the same today. Again and again his father tried to create conversation. But Josh said very little. His suffering had reduced him to short, labored utterances.

Josh watched the lake come into view as they arrived, their car slowing to a stop at the edge of a dead-end road at Good Harbor Bay.

It was Josh who had come up with this idea to spread her ashes at Good Harbor Bay. The two of them stood in the sand and took turns casting the ashes of his mother. Then they went knee-deep in Lake Michigan and did the same. Josh had remembered the night he and his mother paged through the photo albums. He would never forget that evening at home in the living room with her—never forget how much she loved this very special place.

Unknown to them, on a bluff high above the bay, an old man with wild white hair and bib overalls stood within a thicket of maples, observing them through binoculars. And then Grandpa Ogden wept.

7
GRANDPA'S CABIN

Josh and his father walked out of the water and turned around to face Good Harbor Bay. Josh returned his arm to the sling and felt a sharp pain. It felt almost good compared to the pain he felt in his heart as he watched the waves draw his mother's ashes into the lake, as he watched her become one with the water.

As his father wheeled their Mercedes around, Josh twisted in his seat to look out the rear window, holding on to the view as long as he could. They were headed for Grandpa Ogden's place. Within a few minutes they were winding up Grandpa's two-track. As they got out of the car at the cabin, they saw him walking out of the woods, rubbing his bloodshot eyes. A chill ran up Josh's spine when he saw his grandpa, even though he'd seen him just a week before at the funeral. He wore denim bib overalls with no shirt underneath, his hairy white arms and shoulders protruding from under the straps. The hair on his head matched the white beard that flowed down to the middle of his chest.

His mother always said Grandpa Ogden stuck out in a crowd. He sure didn't look like anyone Josh would see back home. At the funeral Grandpa had worn a wrinkled white shirt with a clip-on tie that kept falling off and a mismatched suit. It seemed Grandpa had mistakenly switched the trousers from two suits. Or maybe he just didn't care. Grandpa had been very quiet, but kind. It was the only time Josh could remember his grandpa having made the trip downstate. He had driven his 1961 Chevrolet Apache pickup truck by himself. Josh's father had told him that it took a lot of courage for Grandpa to drive to the city that day.

Josh, clutching his father's hand, walked toward Grandpa. Grandpa's unkempt hair and long beard blew wildly in the breeze. He looks like Father Time, Josh thought, staring at the oddity of this old man.

"Hi, Dad. What's the matter with your eyes?" Josh's father asked.

"Oh, it's just hay fever or ragweed, I guess." Grandpa held up the binoculars he was holding. "I was just out lookin' at birds."

Grandpa extended his hand to Josh, and when Josh

shook it, it felt like a bear paw. "So how ya doin', Cubby. I'm sorry for you. I'm so sorry," he said.

There's that "Cubby" nickname, Josh thought to himself, but answered softly, "I'm doing all right."

The three of them climbed onto the porch. Josh noticed a bad odor. His grandpa stunk. His father and grandpa hugged each other, and then the three of them went into the cabin. Josh and his father looked at each other; they could not believe what they saw. Empty cans littered the floor. Dishes were piled everywhere. No wall divided the living area from the kitchen; the cabin was too small to need one. There was a sort of path connecting the two spaces. On both sides of the path there were piles of old newspapers, empty bags, kindling wood, and whatever else Grandpa had dropped and not picked up. The debris totally covered the wood floor except for the path. There was even a rake lying beside the mess.

The only thing that wasn't a mess was a neat little bed next to the wood stove, with a dog sitting up in it.

"Where'd the dog come from Dad?" Noah asked.

"Found her. Her name's Peach."

"Oh. Gee Dad, the place needs a little attention, doesn't it," Noah said.

A little attention! Josh thought as he swatted at a fly that was buzzing his head. More like tear the place down and start over!

"Yes, yes," Grandpa replied. "I was goin' to get around to it today, but I didn't. I've been feelin' a little punky lately."

Noah glanced down at the rake. "So what were you going to do? Rake the floor?"

"Yes. Yes I was," Grandpa answered. "I thought that would be a good start."

Then Noah asked, "Say Dad, do you mind if we stay here tonight with you? Josh and I will sleep in the loft."

Josh looked up at his father like he'd lost his mind. Sleep here tonight? Why not sleep at the motel with the swimming pool like they always had? Was his father kidding?

Grandpa smiled and got excited and said, "Sure, sure, you betcha."

The last time Josh had visited the cabin was after Grandma's funeral. Relatives, friends, and neighbors gathered for a potluck dinner in honor of Grandma. The inside of the cabin seemed clean and tidy, although a little dark because of the log walls. There was no television set, so Josh spent most of the day outside hitting golf balls back and forth across the front yard, away from the grownups, who were inside talking and eating.

Out back, there was a flower bed along the rear of the cabin, edged with Petoskey stones. A gravel path ran back to a lumber mill attached to a barn, and a horse paddock. Josh did not like being back there because of the horse flies and black flies that bit him when he got near the barn, and the bloodthirsty mosquitoes that swarmed him when he got near the woods. He hated bugs. And he didn't want to go near the barn because he gagged on the smell of horse poop, although he was impressed and a little scared when Grandpa showed him the two big draft horses in their stalls. They seemed so huge he couldn't understand how a person could handle them. After the potluck dinner, Josh and his dad and mom stayed at the motel with the swimming pool and then drove home the next morning.

Josh watched his father scan the cabin. "Well, let's get our gear out of the car and put it in the loft," he said.

Oh no, it was true, Josh thought to himself. Dad wasn't kidding; we are going to sleep here. This is going to be a long and scary night. He quickly ran out the door. It was refreshing to be outside and alone.

"The cub doesn't say too much, does he?" Grandpa said to Josh's father.

"It's not you," his dad replied, "it's because of the accident. He's quieter right now. Put up with it. Give him some time to get used to you and the place. I'm going to go help him get the gear out of the car."

Josh was standing next to the car as his father unloaded the luggage. His arm hurt too much to help, but he asked his father, "Why are we staying here? This place is a dump. Grandpa smells like garbage."

"Shh," his father whispered, looking up to see if Grandpa had heard. "Grandpa needs help. Can't you tell?"

Josh shrugged his shoulders and replied "I guess so." Then he asked, "What's a loft?"

"It's above the living room," his father said. "It used to be my bedroom."

"I didn't see the stairs," said Josh.

"There aren't any. There's a ladder we have to get out from under Grandpa's bed. It's made out of tree poles. Not with the bark on them. It's smooth and sturdy. Don't worry about it," his father said.

Josh thought about this. The only ladder he had ever climbed was a small stepladder inside his house.

His father carried their baggage inside and then dragged the ladder from under the bed, tilted it against the loft, and climbed up with their gear. Josh climbed up the ladder using his left arm. Kind of neat climbing this ladder, he thought to himself, when he reached the loft.

His father turned on the nightstand light next to the twin bed. "This was my bedroom my whole life when I was a boy like you," he said. "This bedroom and this cabin were my home."

The light cast dark, scary shadows on the log walls. His father pointed to the other end of the loft. "You see that small tree-pole bed over there? That'll be your bed. Grandpa built that one for me, and when I grew out of it, he bought me the twin bed."

They slid the rustic wooden bed across the loft floor and arranged the beds side by side, then unpacked their clothing and climbed down the ladder to join Grandpa below. Josh's father picked some old newspapers off the sofa so they could sit down. He looked around for some-place to put them, and then gave up and dropped them on the floor.

They talked with Grandpa for about an hour. Josh's father asked several questions about Grandpa's health.

"How are your teeth, Dad?"

"I still got most of 'em, and they don't hurt," Grandpa answered.

Josh just sat quietly listening and wondering, so when is Dad going to ask Grandpa the last time he took a shower? Soon after this point Josh's father yawned a fake yawn, and said, "Well, I guess I'll head to the kitchen and have a glass of water and call it a night. How about it, Josh?"

Josh nodded okay. They tiptoed through the debris to the kitchen and looked for a clean glass but couldn't find one. When his dad opened a cabinet door, mouse droppings scattered everywhere.

Finally, they located a clean old Mason jar with the lid fastened to its top so no mice had been in it. They drank heartily, but the well water tasted strange. His dad picked up one of the plates from the pile on the counter and examined it. He picked up another and another. All the plates on the counter had dried food stuck to them, top and bottom.

"Why do these plates have food stuck on both sides?" Josh's dad called in to Grandpa.

"Well, after I got done eating off the top of the plate, I just flipped it over and ate off the bottom the next time. Two meals off one plate. Pretty good idea, huh?" Grandpa answered. More like pretty disgusting idea, Josh thought.

"But I can't eat off plates anymore. I can only use a bowl and spoon. It's my hands. They're stiff. Those plates have been there fer a long while. I just use one big bowl now and a big spoon. I keep 'em both clean."

Then the three of them headed for bed, Grandpa retreating alone into the bedroom he had shared with Grandma for more than fifty years.

8
THE SLEEPOVER

〜〜〜〜〜

As Josh lay down in the old bed he sank deeply into the mattress. It felt more like a hammock than a bed, and it squeaked when he rolled on his side to face his father. His father noticed the odd look on Josh's face and whispered, "The springs on the bed are old and soft. They were old and soft when Grandpa first put them in. Believe me, I understand. I slept on that squeaky thing for years."

"This bed's really narrow," Josh whispered. It was so narrow he had to keep his arms tight against his body.

"You'll get used it," his father whispered. "Just go to sleep and forget about it."

But they couldn't sleep. Both tossed and turned for a long time. Josh heard strange noises. Scratching noises.

"What's that noise?" Josh whispered, aware his father was still awake.

"Mice," his father whispered back.

Mice! Oh great, he thought. Now I'm going to have mice crawling all over me all night. This is getting really creepy.

After a while his dad whispered, "It would take a crew of people to clean this place. Heck, it would take two days just to clean Grandpa. We haven't got time. His mind seems fine; he just needs help keeping the place up."

Josh slept restlessly through the night. He woke up, it seemed, every ten minutes. Were those mice he felt under the covers? His thoughts strayed to cartoons he'd seen— mice dancing and playing, sitting in a row, staring down at him from the headboard. His imagination raced.

Josh awakened in the gray dawn that was beginning to light the inside of the cabin. He heard Grandpa walking around, so he woke his father and they climbed down the ladder. All three shared what road food was left over in the cooler from the trip up north, and then they walked out to the barn. Josh and his dad watched as Grandpa fed and watered his two draft horses. They seemed in better shape than Grandpa. Grandpa loved his horses and wanted to stay in the barn and clean up the manure. Just then one of the horses pooped and the pile plopped on the ground in front of Josh. He thought he was going to puke.

He and his father went back inside and left Grandpa to clean up after the horses.

"So what do we do?" Josh asked.

"You can't do anything with that arm and shoulder of yours," his dad said, looking around the cabin. "This is hopeless. The best I can do today is get these dishes washed and wipe down the kitchen counters and wood stove."

"Wood stove?" Josh asked.

His father explained that Grandpa heated the place with logs he cut from the trees on his property. Wood was plentiful and cheap, but cutting and splitting it and then feeding the fire took a lot of effort. " 'Heat you twice,' your Grandpa always said. 'First when you're cuttin' it, and then again when you burn it.' "

As Josh stared at the wood stove curiously, his father said, "First we need to get these dishes in the sink and let them soak in hot soapy water to loosen the crud that's stuck on 'em. While the dishes are soaking, we'll go to Leland and buy about a month's worth of food. There's hardly anything for him to eat and he's losing weight. I don't even want to guess what he's been eating."

Josh and his father drove to Leland and returned with bags full of groceries. His father and grandfather worked all day scrubbing everything in the kitchen. Josh watched them work for a while, and then he went outside, feeling lucky his injuries kept him out of doing all that hard and nasty work. He didn't want to touch anything in the cabin. He had never really done housework before, except maybe climbing a stepladder to change a light bulb.

Late in the afternoon his father and grandfather completed their scrubbing and put the groceries away. Exhausted, Josh's father loaded up the Mercedes and prepared to leave for home. Grandpa was still a mess. There was no time left to scrub him up, too. They each said goodbye to Grandpa from the side of the car.

"Hey, Dad, I bought a bunch of soap. It's in the bathroom. Try using some," Josh's father said before they pulled out of the drive.

Grandpa laughed. "Much obliged. Much obliged fer the help, fellas. Be seein' ya, Cubby."

As they drove home, they both were quiet. Josh looked at his father, still hot and sweaty, and thought, Boy, now Dad stinks as bad as Grandpa.

His father had not said a word for many miles. He suddenly broke the silence. "I don't know what to do about your grandpa. He has always been eccentric but meticulous in what he does. Sloppy behavior is not one of his traits. He just can't keep up with his life now."

Then his father added, "Your Grandma was his partner in life, and they helped take care of each other for over fifty years."

"Like you and Mom?"

"Exactly. But I can't think about that now. We did the best we could while we were there."

"Why don't you want to think about it?"

"Why?" his father replied. "I have to go back to work in two weeks. They'll want me back in New York, but I'm going to ask them if I can work out of the Birmingham office for a while, where I worked before the transfer. That's as far as I can look ahead. I have to get organized. Hire a nanny, house maintenance workers, maids, and whatever else. Get everything organized before you go back to school."

"But what about Grandpa?"

Josh's father did not answer. He just rubbed his forehead and frowned.

9
THE PROMISE

In the weeks following his return from Good Harbor Bay, Josh watched as his father tried to get the household back into a working routine. Just before his father was scheduled to go back to work, Josh met the nanny who his father had hired to take care of him. When she left, Josh and his father went into the living room and sat down across from each other. Josh watched his father bow his head, rub his eyes, and, finally, look up at him in an unusual, sad way.

"Dad, are you having a bad time?" Josh asked.

After a long pause his dad answered. "I don't know how to deal with all this."

"Deal with what?" asked Josh.

"All this stuff I'm trying to do around here is just haunting me. You know, Josh, parents can be frightened when new challenges come up for the first time. I've got a lot of them right now. That's what's haunting me."

His father suddenly changed the subject. "Did you change the bandages on your arms this morning? You know what the doctor said about infection from the burns. You have to keep it up until they heal over. I want to look at them tonight."

"Yes, I changed them," Josh replied. "They're just about all healed. Do you like the nanny?"

"No . . . I mean, yes. But she's just an employee to take care of you while I'm at work. She's not your mom. You know, Mom did a lot that I took for granted. But besides all this busy stuff . . ." he paused and then winced. "I just miss her."

Josh watched his father bury his head in his hands again. "I don't want to upset you," his dad said, "but there's something I'm feeling. Maybe you're feeling it, too. The longer Mom is gone I feel her fading from our life, and I don't want that to happen."

Josh got up and sat next to his father. "I don't want her to go away either. It was bad what happened to her. It's not fair. Sometimes when I'm lying in bed at night I get mad. I can't believe that the drunk driver who murdered my mother was not even hurt in the accident. I miss her so much."

"We have to make a promise," Noah said. "We have to vow to never let Mom's voice fade from within us. It doesn't have to be a sad thing. We just have to remember her. Remember the images of her standing with us. Remember her voice when she talked to us. Remember the life we shared with her."

Josh tried to hold back tears, but could not. "We'll keep Mom in our memories like pictures. We can kind of pretend she's standing next to us as we live our life."

10
HOUSE OF NANNIES

Josh woke up early Monday so he could spend some time with his dad before his first day of work at the company's branch office in Birmingham. Josh also wanted to be ready when the nanny showed up.

When she arrived, his dad reintroduced them. She was older and plump. Nothing like his mother. But she seemed pleasant enough. Without a lot of conversation she went to the kitchen and began preparing breakfast. Josh said goodbye to his dad and sat down to eat. It was strange getting his breakfast served by a nanny. Very strange. The only words he could get out were a weak "thank you" as the nanny cleared the table.

He got up and went to his room and watched television. He felt abandoned without his father around. Is this, he asked himself, my new life? Is this the way it will be from now on?

As the summer progressed, his father called him three times a day to see how things were going. Josh always said everything was fine, but it wasn't. He watched television in his room all day, lying on his bed and glancing between the reruns on television and the clock on the nightstand, as he waited for his father to come home. Josh thought about school but wasn't looking forward to going back. Trevor and other friends sent text messages that vibrated on his cell phone, but Josh did not answer. Then the text messages stopped. He even missed the sound of the music students' violins. Wish I had taken lessons myself from Mom, he thought. It would have made her so happy.

Josh was certain his father was going to spring the news any day that they would be moving to New York. Was he going to New York to live in a house of nannies? Or was he going live in the house of nannies here? Either way, he imagined his father was going to become a shadow, a ghost in his life who would appear and then disappear. It had started already. This morning his father had left without saying goodbye. Josh had tossed and turned most of the night, then had fallen into a deep sleep until eleven o'clock in the morning when the nanny woke him with a knock on the door.

"Joshua, your father called and wanted you to know

that he'd be very busy for the rest of the day and would
be home late."

Another day of abandonment, he thought. Sounds like
Dad is really getting into his work again. Josh watched
television all day, dozing off and on between shows.

That evening at around six-thirty, the nanny knocked
on his door again. "Joshua, your father called again. He's
on his way home and bringing a pizza. Your father said
it was okay for me to leave. He should be here in half
an hour."

Josh shuffled out of his room and went downstairs to
the refrigerator and pulled out a Coke. He sat down at
the kitchen table. He felt very alone. Hmm, pizza, Josh
thought. Dad knows pizza's my favorite meal. He must be
planning to patch things up and make everything okay
after not calling all day and coming home so late. Through

past experience Josh knew his father's various ways of smoothing over long days or long business trips, and he was getting tired of it.

I bet I'm going to find out tonight which house of nannies it will be—New York or Birmingham. It's probably the big speech about New York and how it's going to be so wonderful and exciting.

An hour later Josh heard the garage door open. His dad entered the kitchen, carrying the pizza. Except for a short "Hi," neither said a word. They sat down together and started eating. Finally his father said, "Aren't you going to ask me how my day went at work? What I did?"

Instantly Josh thought to himself, Here comes New York, I can feel it. "Okay," he asked cautiously, "How'd it go? What did you do at work?"

"I quit."

Josh dropped his slice of pizza. "Quit what?"

"I quit my job. I told the nanny she didn't have to come anymore. But I told her not to tell you."

Josh's eyes brightened. "No way. You're going to be here tomorrow?"

"Yup. Tomorrow and the day after that and many days after that. New York, Birmingham, Chicago, or wherever—it wouldn't work for us. Careers and money just aren't that important to me anymore. It's taken me a few weeks to come to grips with it, but it's just us that matters."

Josh was stunned . . . speechless. Just when he thought he had things figured out, everything turned upside down.

His father's lip quivered a little as he continued. "You know Josh, we can't forget how Mom spent her whole life serving others—mainly you and me, but music students, too."

"I know."

"Remember the night we talked about not wanting Mom's spirit to fade?"

"I'll never forget it."

"Well, I think her voice, her life, is speaking to us now. To serve others."

Josh tore into the pizza, as though eating might help make sense of all the thoughts racing through his head.

"But we have a big mountain to climb," his dad continued. "It's going to be difficult for you. It's going to be difficult for me. We are going to serve others, right?"

"Yeah, I guess," Josh said. "But who?"

Josh thought for a few minutes. His father sat in silence, spinning his slice of pizza. Oh, no, Josh said to himself as an image popped in his head. Serving others. What was his father going to do? What was he up to? Was his father going off the deep end? Were they going to live in huts and serve the poor?

"Grandpa," his dad answered in a single, terrifying word.

What? Josh asked himself. Was Grandpa moving in with them? Was Grandpa going to stink up the place? He would scare the neighbors. He would embarrass him in front of his friends. But he didn't dare say what he was thinking because he did not want to give his father any ideas in case he was wrong. So he just asked, "What are you, I mean we, going to do?"

"I talked to Grandpa on the telephone. Actually every day since I went back to work. We have talked long and hard. We have to help him or he's going to rot and die alone up there. Do you want to help him?"

Josh thought quickly, decided there was no other answer, and said, "I guess."

His father breathed in deeply, clearly relieved at Josh's response. "Okay. I want you to believe in me. I'm trying to do the right thing. You're not ready to go back to school. You know that and I know that. I'm going to homeschool you . . . and I want us to move to the Leelanau Peninsula. To Good Harbor Bay. To live with Grandpa in the cabin. Just the three of us."

Josh's eyes widened and his heart sank. "Live with Grandpa in that dirty log cabin?"

"Yes."

Josh started thinking about the filth and stink and then about bugs and horse poop.

"We'll clean the cabin and Grandpa," his dad said. "We'll

make it our new home. We'll make it a very comfortable place to live. Just the three of us. We have nothing here anymore. You walk to the kitchen, then back to your bedroom, and that's all. You'd do the same thing in New York. The only good thing that we have to remember about this place is that your mother walked here. And, if you think about it, we'll be closer to Mom at Good Harbor Bay."

One minute Josh's spirit had been soaring; now it was crashing back to earth. "I don't want to live there!" he screamed. "Can't Grandpa just live here? I'm not going! I'll go and live with Trevor or somebody!"

11
BLISTERS

Josh had given up trying to talk his father out of moving north. It was clear his father was going to make the move no matter what. So here he was in this dump in the woods—shut in his own little world like a prisoner.

It seemed like the wilderness compared to Birmingham. No friends. Not a swimming pool or neighbor in sight. And Josh had all the joy of being woken up by a snowball lobbed into his bed by his grandfather.

He climbed down the wooden ladder and sat down to breakfast.

"When you're done eating, take your plate to the sink and go out and help your grandpa clean the barn," his father said.

Josh did not answer as he continued to stir his food.

"Did you hear me, Josh?"

"Yeah, I'm coming."

As soon as his father and grandfather went outside Josh scampered over to the computer and checked his e-mail. Josh did not have his cell phone anymore because his father said he didn't need it. The computer was his last link to the old world. When he had learned he was going to have to move here, he had started communicating with Trevor again. In one of his messages Josh pleaded for help. He had asked Trevor to ask his parents if he could move in with them.

S.O.S. . . . I'M A HURTIN DUDE . . . NEED HELP, he had typed.

OK BY ME, BUT MY M&D SAID NO, Trevor had e-mailed back. NOT REALISTIC.

Now, months later, every time he tried to sneak in a phone call from his grandfather's telephone to Trevor's cell phone, it rang and rang and went to voice mail. If he called Trevor's house it was about the same, except sometimes one of his parents answered to say that Trevor was not home. Josh was convinced he was being avoided.

Josh began to turn off the laptop. The e-mails had stopped. His communication with his old life was over.

The front door opened. "Josh, get away from that computer and go help your grandpa," said his father.

"All right, I'm comin' out," Josh answered.

His father had always been big on discipline, but it

seemed he was becoming unusually strict with him now. Josh knew his father thought he was way too negative about everything, but what could he do? He hated being here. And now he had lost his friends back home. He was alone.

Josh put on his coat and boots and headed across the barnyard. He entered the barn, picked up a flat shovel, and started shoveling the manure toward the barn door. His hands were beginning to hurt again.

His grandfather walked over and started shoveling next to him, and said, "Yer pa and me are goin' to make a man out of ya yet, aren't we."

Josh lost his temper, ripping off his gloves and yelling, "Look at all these blisters on my hands!"

"That's just baby fat. It'll wear off."

Josh threw down his shovel just as his father drove by with the snowplow. Noah stopped and got out of the truck.

"Baby fat!" Josh yelled at Grandpa. "I don't know what you're talkin' about. What are you tryin' to do? Tease me into getting mad? Well, I'm mad!"

"Cubby doesn't cotton to me, does he, Noah?" Grandpa Oggy said to Josh's dad.

"Cotton to you?" Josh yelled. "I don't know what the heck you're talking about and don't call me Cubby and I'm sick of smelling and shoveling horse poop! Look at these blisters on my hands from all the shoveling! All you two do is tell me to grab a shovel! Baby fat! Now I've heard it all! I've had it!" He picked up his shovel and threw it as far as he could.

"What's all yer grousing about! Hold your potatoes, boy, don't talk to me or your pa that way!" Grandpa Oggy shouted back.

"You can't tell me what to say or do. You're not my dad!" Josh yelled back.

"You're bein' a bad apple, boy! If it were up to me I'd . . ."

Noah interrupted, "Stop it, both of you! That's enough!"

Then his father grabbed Josh by the shoulder and yanked him close to his face. "I've lost my patience with you, Josh," he shouted. "The next time I hear you complain about shoveling manure, or even complain about the smell of it, you're going to shovel by yourself for a week! Treat us with respect and you'll get treated with respect. It's your choice."

His father released his grip on Josh's coat. Josh had never seen him this angry. It scared him.

As Josh picked up his shovel, he could hear his father and grandfather arguing as they walked toward the house. It sounded like his father wasn't too happy with Grandpa Oggy's behavior either. He kept hearing Grandpa Oggy saying, "Yeah, but Noah he was . . . yeah, but Noah . . ." all the way back to the cabin. As he started shoveling again he thought of running away, but he had no idea where he would run. He started to cry.

Suddenly his dad turned around, telling Grandpa Oggy he'd meet him in the cabin in a few minutes. He walked back to Josh.

"We need to talk, Josh."

"About what?" Josh snarled, not looking up as he continued shoveling.

"Settle down. Take a couple of deep breaths. Just listen to me for a few minutes. We all need to catch some deep breaths. I lost my temper, too."

Josh stopped working. As he lifted his head up to face his father, tears were still running down his cheeks.

Noah said, "Your grandfather forgets the big picture. I think maybe I have, too. I have some of the same feelings you have. I miss your mom as much as you do. This life we have now is just as strange and difficult for me as it is for you. Your Grandpa Oggy has always thought that hard work can somehow shake a person into forgetting whatever problems are going on inside. That's what made me run away from this place and never come back when I went away to college. He's set in his ways. Always been this way."

"So what are you saying? You hate it here as much as I do? Then let's get out of here."

"What I'm trying to say is I don't have all the answers. I'm feeling my way through this and trying to do the right thing, but I'm making mistakes along the way. Grandpa Oggy forgets that we came here to help him. We're supposed to be helping each other. Without you and me, he'd be struggling to continue living."

"He doesn't seem to care about how I feel," Josh complained.

"Yes he does, in his own way. His behavior just doesn't express it. He probably still has the same feelings about missing Grandma as we do about Mom."

"I know, but it just seems like it isn't just you and me anymore. It seems more like Grandpa and you are a team, and then there's me."

"This isn't a game of Grandpa Oggy and me against you. I brought you here because I thought the change of atmosphere might help us while we help your grandfather. Maybe we just need to be a little more laid back about all these chores. You know what I mean?"

"I'm for that," Josh said. "But talk to him like you did to me, Dad. He bugs me."

"I will, right now. He can bug me, too. I'm going to go back to the cabin and try to teach that old dog some new tricks."

12
GRANDPA'S TRUCK

Josh studied at his desk in the silence of the cabin. The only sounds were the faint tick of clocks and snapping firewood burning in the wood stove. His father had asked him if he wanted to go to town with him, but Josh had said no. These late afternoons were the only time of day he felt relaxed. He enjoyed losing himself in his studying.

The tag-team, boot-camp work regimen with his father and grandfather had stopped since the blowup of few days ago. He was just beginning to feel close to his father again, but it had only been a short time. He hoped the change would last.

His grandfather had not spoken to him at all, but Josh thought that was probably because Grandpa just wanted to be left alone.

He looked up from his book when he heard the front

door open. His grandfather stepped inside, kicked his boots off, and walked over to the wood stove, rubbing his hands to warm them. Josh looked back down at his book, irritated by the interruption. Neither of them spoke.

Finally his grandfather said, "Josh?"

Without looking up from his book, Josh said, "What?" and then realized Grandpa had not called him Cubby.

"My hands aren't workin' so good today. It's the rheumatism or arthritis. I was wonderin' if you could drive me down to the mailbox to fetch the mail. Before he went to town yer pa told me to go down and pick it up. He's expectin' a big paycheck. He didn't want the mail to sit in the box all day until he gets home."

Josh looked up at him and said, "I can't drive the truck. I'm only twelve."

"There's no law that says you can't drive my truck on my property. Yer pa did when he was your age."

Josh stood up and said, "Sure, but I don't know how to drive."

"It's easy. I'll show ya."

They put their coats and boots on and walked out to the truck. Josh climbed in on the driver's side and his grandfather took the passenger side.

"This is a 1961 three-on-the-tree Chevrolet Apache pickup. They call it a three-on-the-tree because the manual three-speed stick shift is up on the post. The 'tree' is connected to the steerin' wheel," his grandfather said.

Josh stared at the shifter.

"I bought her new that year for cash. That was a big deal for me back then."

Josh looked at the dashboard. There was only a speedometer, an engine temperature light, and an oil gauge. Down next to the steering wheel there were two pull knobs: one had the letter *C* written on it, the other had a *T*. There was no radio or anything else.

"Look down at the pedals. You see, there's three. The one on the left is the clutch. The middle one's the brake, and the one to the right is the gas. Push down on the clutch with your left foot."

Josh edged to the front of the seat and pushed his foot down as hard as he could.

"You gotta push that clutch in all the way so you don't grind the gears. You'll get the idea," said Grandpa Oggy. "While you're pushin', can ya see over the steerin' wheel?"

Josh peeked over the steering wheel. "Barely." His nose was about even with the top of the wheel.

"That's close enough as long as you can see out the windshield," Grandpa said. "Now fix the rearview mirror so ya can see what's behind ya."

Josh adjusted the mirror.

"Now pull out the C-knob all the way—that's the choke. Then pull out the T-knob about halfway—that's the engine throttle. This truck's way easier than your pa's truck. I don't like driving his truck. Too many gadgets."

"Yeah, but in his truck all you have to do is turn the key and put it in drive from what I've seen," Josh said. "You have to do a lot of stuff to start this truck."

"I guess it's what yer used to," Grandpa said. "Anyways, that shifter there is where the three gears are. First, second, and third makes three. You start in first gear. Push in the clutch and pull the shift in and all the way down into first gear and turn the key."

Josh pushed in the clutch and shifted down into first gear. He turned the key and smiled when the truck sputtered a few times and then started. But just as it was starting to run, he forgot about the clutch and let it out. The truck jumped ahead and stalled.

"That's okay, Josh. I still do that once in a while. Start her again."

Josh pressed down hard on the clutch and started the truck. Everything went well this time, but the truck began to sputter in about a minute.

"Push in the choke and throttle all the way now. The engine's warmed up. You only have to use them at the beginning when the engine's cold."

The engine calmed to idle.

"Okay, now give the truck some gas and let the clutch out real slow. It's easy. You'll get the hang of it real quick."

Josh gave the truck some gas, slowly releasing the clutch, and on the first try they moved ahead. He looked over at Grandpa, who was wearing a big smile.

"You gotta do all the clutchin' and shiftin' at the same time lookin' to where yer goin', Josh."

He and Grandpa drove back and forth in the part of the barnyard that had been plowed. Sometimes the truck would jerk forward and quit when Josh tried to change gears. Other times it lurched into gear and picked up speed. Before long it was starting to feel natural.

"Anyways, you got the hang of it," Grandpa said, "so let's head down to the mailbox. You gotta drive this truck slow with the snow chains on the back tires."

They started down the winding two-track. As they rounded a small bend in the road, Josh yanked the steering wheel hard to the right, but the truck kept on going straight, headed for a clump of trees. Josh stomped on the brake, at the same time pushing in the clutch, and the truck skidded to a stop just short of the tree and a snowbank.

"That's okay, yer drivin' slow. That's why you didn't hit anything," Grandpa laughed, completely unconcerned that his truck had nearly plowed into the trees. "If you'd hit the tree that woulda been all right though," he added gently. "Sometimes a person makes mistakes. Even when yer growed up ya make mistakes. That's how all the rest of these dents got in the truck—from me makin' mistakes and hittin' trees. The rusted dents are the oldest. The unrusted dents I made in the last couple years. Just back her up and do 'er again."

Josh thought, is he trying to say in his own way that he is sorry and makes mistakes? Maybe.

After his grandfather had retrieved the mail, Josh asked how he was going to turn around without going into the street.

"Oh, I guess it doesn't matter if we go out on the pavement," Grandpa answered. "There's never any traffic out here. Just turn right and drive down about a quarter mile and we'll turn around. Nothin's gonna happen. I did the same thing with yer pa."

Now Josh was a little scared, but he wanted to do it. He turned right, shifted into second, and watched the speedometer climb to over twenty-five miles per hour. Feeling a bit nervous, he accidentally ground the gears as he shifted into third. As they cruised down the road, he struggled to keep the truck in the right lane, occasionally drifting to the other side. Oh, man, he thought, I sure am lucky there's no traffic coming the other way.

"You gotta get used to the steerin' wheel. It's got a lot of play in it," said Grandpa Oggy.

"Yeah, so I noticed."

Then Josh looked out of the rearview mirror. Out of nowhere a car appeared within a few feet of the back of the truck. And when he saw red and blue lights flashing, blood rushed to his head and his heart began to pump wildly. It was the sheriff. Josh could hear the loud, piercing sound of the siren. Grandpa Oggy turned and looked out the rear window.

"Uh-oh, now we got big-time real trouble. Pull over, Josh. I hope it's not one of those pesky young deputies tryin' to make a name fer himself."

Josh pulled over and jerked to a stop. His whole body was shaking.

The deputy walked over to Josh's window and tapped on it, signaling for him to open it. Josh cranked the window down. It was difficult to crank the handle because his arm shook so much.

"Good afternoon," said the deputy. "Driver's license and registration, please."

"I don't have those. I'm twelve," Josh answered.

"Twelve?" said the deputy. The deputy bent down and looked into the truck. "That you Oggy?"

Grandpa looked over at the deputy and said, "Yep, hi Bart."

"Oggy, can I see you in back of the truck? Son, turn off the truck and give me the keys."

Josh handed the deputy the keys as his grandfather climbed out. In the rearview mirror he saw Grandpa and the deputy talking. He knew for sure he was going to jail.

His father was going to kill him. How much time would he have to spend in jail? he wondered. A year? Maybe he would never be able to get a license when he was old enough. What else could go wrong? Just when he thought life was getting a little better, this had to happen. "I'm jinxed!" he said out loud.

Then he saw his grandfather approaching the truck as the deputy got back into his police car. Grandpa opened the driver's-side door and said, "Slide over, Josh."

"I thought your hands hurt too much to drive? And what's going to happen to me?"

"My hands are feelin' better," Grandpa smirked as he started the truck and made a U-turn. The deputy smiled at Oggy as they drove past him.

"What's goin' to happen? What's goin' to happen is you, me, yer pa, and Bart and his boy are goin' ice fishin' on Saturday, that's what goin' to happen. Bart's got a big ice shanty on North Lake Leelanau."

"Really?"

Grandpa shifted into third gear. "We were lucky today. That was Bart Bartelli. Yer pa and him went to high school together. He's got a boy about yer age, I guess. His boy's name's Jake. We're goin' to have some fun. Yer pa told me years ago Bart Bartelli's nickname was 'Black Bart Bartelli' because he was the toughest kid in high school. Nobody messed with him."

Grandpa Oggy downshifted into second gear and turned onto their two-track.

"You mean I'm not going to have to go to jail?" Josh asked.

"Naw, it's over and done," Grandpa said.

After a moment Josh's panic subsided and he began to focus on what Grandpa had said. "How do you ice fish? What kind of fish are we going to catch?"

"Ya use minnies fer bait to catch perch and walleye."

"Mini what to catch perch and walleye?"

"It's not 'mini' anything. It's 'minnies.' Minnows. Some folks around here call minnows 'minnies.' Probably only the old-timers now, I guess."

"Oh, like a nickname."

"I dunno, I guess. Well, did ya have fun today?" Grandpa Oggy asked.

"It's fun now. It wasn't so fun a few minutes ago."

"Yep, we were lucky it was Black Bart."

"Do you call him that to his face?"

Grandpa Oggy hesitated for a second, and then answered, "I used to, but maybe I should stop callin' him that. That nickname's from a long time ago. I guess I'll call him Bart. He's a nice man. I hope you like his boy."

13
ICE FISHING

As promised, Noah, Grandpa, and Mr. Bartelli took Josh and Jake to North Lake Leelanau the following Saturday morning. The two pickup trucks pulled up at the edge of the lake and the five of them piled out, squinting into the sun. The sun shone brightly in a clear blue sky, which was very unusual for northern Michigan at that time of the year.

Mr. Bartelli and Jake pulled down the tailgate of their pickup and unloaded two handmade wooden sleds with wooden boxes attached to the top. The five of them filled the boxes with ice-fishing poles, ice scoops, a couple of heavy steel poles with a sharp edge on one end they called "spuds," two buckets of bait minnows, and snacks that Josh, his father, and Grandpa had pitched in. Then they walked out on the ice pulling the sleds toward the shanty.

Josh was cold when he left the truck. The sun had melted the top of the deep snow, making a thin crust that he broke through with each step. By the time he'd reached the ice shanty, he had worked up a sweat.

Mr. Bartelli unlocked the padlock on the door of the wooden ice shanty. Jake and his father transferred the gear and hung it on hooks fastened to the inside of the shanty walls. Josh wanted to join in but he didn't know quite what to do, so he simply observed their moves so he would be ready for the next time.

Mr. Bartelli took kindling wood that was piled at the side of the shanty and built a fire in the wood stove inside. Soon brown smoke began to rise out of the shanty's smoke-stack from on top of the roof.

"Most people today use propane stoves to keep them warm inside because it's easier," Mr. Bartelli explained. "But being a policeman, I've had the sad experience on my police calls, more than once, of folks being asphyxi-ated by improper ventilation or malfunctioning propane stoves. I'll stick to wood!"

The floor of the shanty was also wood. Grandpa joined Mr. Bartelli inside the shanty and lifted a big trap door in the middle, exposing a three-foot by three-foot sheet of ice underneath. Grandpa and Mr. Bartelli then chopped around the outside edge of the ice with the spuds as the boys and Noah watched from outside.

Once the men were done chopping around the hole, the chunk of ice broke free and floated in place.

"How are you going to get that big piece of ice out of the hole?" Josh wanted to know. "It's too big and thick to lift out."

"You push it under the water and slide it under the ice with the spuds," Mr. Bartelli answered. "The important thing to remember is always keep the rope that's attached to the top of the spud wrapped around your hand so if you lose your grip on the spud you don't drop it in the lake."

Josh watched the two men push down from each end of the ice chunk and slide it beneath the ice under the floorboards.

"Okay, let's get inside and scoop the slush out of the hole," Jake said to Josh. "But before you go in, take off your coat, 'cause it's going to get hot inside with the stove going."

Jake took off his coat and hung it on one of the nails driven into the outside of the shanty. Josh did the same.

They went inside. Jake took two ice scoops that hung from the walls and handed one to Josh. "Now we have to scoop the ice slush out of the hole so we have clear vision in the water," instructed Jake. "Watch." Jake scooped the slush and flung it outside the open door of the shanty onto the ice.

Easy enough, Josh thought, but he was a little nervous staring down the hole into the water, afraid he'd fall in and disappear under the shanty like the big ice chunk. Slowly he got used to the new surroundings and joined in. The first scoop he flung out was bad timing. As he threw the slush out the door, Mr. Bartelli walked in front of the door opening and got splattered by Josh.

"Sorry Mr. Bartelli," Josh said apologetically in a soft voice.

"Don't worry about it, Josh. It was just an accident. Okay, you guys can have the shanty to yourselves. We're going to spud some holes next to you and fish outside in the sun," said Mr. Bartelli.

When Josh and Jake had cleared the slush from the hole, Jake closed the door. It wasn't long before Josh realized just how right Jake had been about the heat. They stripped down to T-shirts and laid their outer garments on the benches. In the darkness of the shanty, the ice and water glowed, illuminated by the sunlight outside. It was so bright they could see the bottom of the lake about eight feet down.

Josh watched as Jake took his fishing pole and let out a little line. He opened a tin box, took out a little split-shot sinker, and put it on the line about a foot up from the hook. Jake bit down on the split-shot to pinch it on the line.

"Isn't that sinker made of lead?" Josh asked. "My mother said you get lead poisoning putting lead in your mouth."

"Yeah, I guess so. But who cares? Me and dad have always done it this way. I don't worry about all that little stuff."

Jake scooped up a minnow from the bucket and hooked it through the back. He attached a bobber about seven feet up the line and dropped the rig in the hole.

"You see," Jake said, "the bobber keeps the minnow about a foot from the bottom. That's about where I like to start. We'll see if the fish like this depth. If they don't we'll bring the minnow up a little by adjusting the bobber."

Jake started to rig a pole for Josh.

"Hey Jake, I'd like to try to do it myself to get the hang of it."

"Okay, have at it."

Josh let some line out of the reel of the pole, took a split-shot out of the tin box, put it on the line, and bit down on it. He licked his lips. His face grimaced slightly at the thought of lead poisoning.

"How's that, Jake?"

"Looks good. By the look on your face you must've thought you were going to drop dead from lead poisoning when you bit down on that shot. My dad says sometimes we get a little too much information going through our heads nowadays."

"Yeah, I know what you mean," Josh said. "My mom read a lot and was always telling me stuff about what's not good for us." He then scooped down in the minnow bucket and pulled up a bunch of wiggling minnows. They were flipping around everywhere. Some wiggled out of the scoop and fell to the floor.

"Put the minnows in the scoop back in the bucket and pick up one of those on the floor and use it," Jake said.

Josh dumped the minnows back in the bucket and tried to grab one of the wiggling minnows on the floor. "Man, these things are slimy and are flipping all over the place. It's hard to get hold of them. They're so little."

"Where do I hook this little thing?" Josh asked after he finally got hold of one.

"Just hook it behind its head underneath its backbone. About in the middle of its back."

Josh squeezed the minnow tight and punched the hook through its back.

"Okay, send it down to the side of mine, put on your

bobber, and let's catch some fish!"

Their bobbers floated quietly on the surface of the water.

Jake scooped up about ten minnows out of the bucket and dropped them into the hole.

"Whoa. Why are you throwing away our minnows?" Josh asked.

"That's called chumming," Jake said. "The extra minnows down there will attract fish closer to our bait, and with any luck, we'll hook some perch and walleye."

Josh stared at the hole intently, hoping for movement on his bobber or the sight of a big perch or walleye swimming up to the chum minnows. After a few minutes, a school of perch slowly came into view in the hole, staring at the minnows.

"Here they come! They're stalking the minnows," Jake said. "It looks like they're hungry and on the hunt."

After a few minutes Josh's bobber sank beneath the surface. He had a fish on the line! "Give your line a little tug," said Jake. "It'll set the hook in the fish's mouth."

Josh pulled back on the line to set the hook and felt a good fish pulling hard. He reeled as fast as he could and eventually brought the fish to the surface.

"Wow, this rod really has the luck built into it," he said, turning to Jake as he watched the perch flopping on the floor. "Now what do I do?"

"First, keep the fish away from the hole so it doesn't

fall back into the lake if it gets off the hook. Now watch this." Jake took the fish into his hands. "See, you have to grab the fish in the front and slide your hands over the fins on top of the fish. If you don't, the fins can poke you." He removed the hook from the perch's mouth and tossed the fish in a bucket.

Before midafternoon they had what Jake called "a good mess of fish" in the five-gallon bucket.

They heard a knock on the door and Jake opened it. His father, Grandpa, and Mr. Bartelli stood outside.

"We're going to go back to the house and start cleaning our catch. We'll pick you boys up around dark and then we'll all go to the house for a fish fry," said Mr. Bartelli.

"How are you doing?" Noah asked.

Josh broke into a big smile. "We got a mess of them, Dad."

"So did we," said Grandpa. "That's why we're goin' back. Otherwise we'll be up all night cleanin' all the fish includin' yers."

"Make sure you're at the edge of the lake at dusk. Don't forget to put down the trap door, and don't fall in. You guys got your flashlights just in case?" asked Mr. Bartelli.

"Yeah, we do," Jake answered.

The door closed and Josh heard the crunching sounds of the men walking away. He liked the feeling of being alone on the ice with Jake. They were quiet for a while when all of a sudden Josh heard a loud crack, like a gunshot. He jumped up from his seat. "What's going on?"

"Aw, that's nothing. It's just the ice expanding and contracting. It happens all the time. We've got plenty of ice underneath us."

"You sure?"

"I'm sure. It's too cold for anything to happen. My dad wouldn't let us come out here if it wasn't. Remember, he's a cop."

Josh settled back down and they began to chatter about everything. They joked and laughed when fish got off their lines. Jake was a year and a half older than Josh, but that didn't seem to matter to either of them. Their personalities clicked. It felt like Jake could easily become Josh's best friend, just like Trevor had been back in the city. But that's about where Jake's similarity to Trevor ended. Jake did not have a cell phone or text messenger or any electronic devices except a computer, which he was not allowed to use unless one of his parents was present. Jake said that deputy sheriffs did not make much money and they couldn't afford electronic gadgets. But he didn't care, he said, because they were just distractions from what he really loved to do—fish and play hockey and football.

But talking with Jake in the ice shanty, strange as that was, seemed much like the conversations Josh had had with his old friends downstate. Jake talked about girls and his school. Josh listened to Jake gripe about his parents and sister—the same old stuff he used to hear back in Birmingham.

Josh talked about the accident with his mother and where he used to live. But he didn't talk about wanting to live there anymore. Because he didn't—it was in the past.

"So what do you want to be when you grow up, Jake?" Josh asked.

"A deputy sheriff," Jake said without hesitation. "But my dad thinks I'm aiming my sights sort of low. What about you?"

Josh thought for a moment. "I dunno. Maybe something to do with finance like my dad."

"What's your dad do?" Jake asked.

"Well, I'm not really sure, but it has something to do with banks and money and he can do it from home. That's kinda cool, I think."

"Yeah, but it sounds like you'd have to go to the city after college and work at a place. You can't just graduate from college and come back up here and start working on a computer at home."

Josh shrugged. "I dunno. But I know I don't want to work downstate in a big city."

"I couldn't spend my life sitting at home in front of a computer. I think that sounds boring, but everybody's different."

"I have plenty of time to think about it," answered Josh. "I'm not going to worry about it now."

It was nearing dusk when Josh and Jake started to put everything into their sled. "I lost count after catching fifteen perch," Josh said, as they slammed the trap door shut.

"I quit counting after ten. But you caught more perch, that's for certain . . . except I eased up because it was your first time," Jake added with a laugh.

"Yeah, right," Josh added. "But you caught the biggest one—a fifteen-inch walleye."

"It was a beauty all right. And our five-gallon bucket is filled." Jake closed the door and snapped on the padlock. "Let's start walking. We'll pull the sled together. It'll be easier."

When they reached the shore, Mr. Bartelli was there waiting in his pickup truck. He drove them to Jake's house and everyone helped clean the fish. They all stood in a line at the counter, including Jake's younger sister, Angelina, who was about Josh's age. She joined right in gutting the fish, then filleting and skinning them. Mrs. Bartelli deep-fried the fish and also pan-fried potatoes and onions together. They all sat down at the kitchen table and ate the fish and potatoes with catsup. The perch and walleye were delicious, like eating French fries, Josh thought. The fish had no bones in them and were crisp and crunchy. It didn't take long before the whole pile was gone. It was nice being with a family, Josh thought. And it was really nice being around a mother.

14
NEW ARRIVALS

Winter finally gave way to spring. The ice disappeared from Lake Leelanau and from the shores of Lake Michigan. Before the ice left, Noah helped Mr. Bartelli haul the ice shanty off the lake. Josh and Jake's ice fishing adventures were over for the year.

But things were stirring back at the cabin. One day Josh noticed Peach was acting peculiar. She was moving her bedding around, pacing, shivering, and panting. She wouldn't eat and began to vomit. Alarmed, Josh found Grandpa Oggy and told him what he had witnessed. "I think she's really sick and she looks awful out of shape," he said.

Grandpa nodded his head without the slightest sign of concern. "Well Josh," he said while running his fingers through his beard, "I'm planning a little surprise for you. A while back I bred Peach to the neighbor's Brittany so we'd have a litter of puppies. Thought you might like the pick of the litter and we could sell the rest off. You're grown up enough now to handle raising a pup."

"No way!" Josh nearly shrieked, overwhelmed at the thought of being a proud "parent" of a new Brittany. "But why's she acting so strange?"

"Just signs of being pregnant. She must be gettin' close to delivery."

Josh broke the news to his father, who was shocked that he hadn't noticed the pregnancy before now and insisted they take Peach to the veterinarian for a checkup. Grandpa said it wasn't necessary. Nature would follow its course, he said, but Noah set up an appointment anyway.

The next day at the vet clinic the veterinarian put her up on an examining table and checked her behind with his latex-gloved fingers. He took a few drops of urine for a sample, drew some blood from a vein in her leg, and left the room.

In a few minutes he returned.

"She's in stage one labor, which lasts about eighteen hours. The reason she's been moving her pillows and blankets and such around, is because she's trying to build a nest. So let her do it. Josh, I want to teach you how to take Peach's temperature rectally," he said with the wink of an eye to Noah. Josh scrunched up his face with a look of disgust.

The veterinarian handed the thermometer to Josh and said, "Insert it about an inch into her rectum and leave it in place for three minutes." Josh grasped the thermometer and carefully, but reluctantly, followed the vet's instructions.

"Very good, Josh. You seem like a natural at this. You can keep the thermometer and take it home. Now, when her temperature falls below 100 degrees she should deliver the puppies within twenty-four hours. She'll most likely take care of herself and the puppies during delivery, but there can be problems. The puppies will be born covered by an amniotic membrane—a sac. Most mother dogs lick the sac rather roughly to tear the membrane off, which stimulates the puppies to breathe and then momma bites off the umbilical cord.

"Now if she doesn't do this you'll have to. You'll have to tear the sac open, clear all membrane and fluid away first from each puppy's nose and mouth, peel the membrane away with a towel, and vigorously rub the pup to stimulate breathing. And then tie a piece of dental floss or thread around the umbilical cord about an inch from each puppy's belly button and cut the cord. I'll give you some reading information with pictures to study up on all this. You have a lot of studying to do fast. If you have any questions call me here or at my home. I'll help you through this, or I can come to your home day or night."

On the way home Peach was struggling and Josh was anxious to get back to the cabin to get everything set up. He was making a plan. He'd sleep in a sleeping bag next to Peach's bedding area and stay up all night to keep an eye on her.

That night Josh was all set up. He had his sleeping bag next to Peach, had read and memorized all the information, and had his scissors, dental floss, towels, and string if he needed them. Before his dad and grandpa went to sleep, he took Peach's temperature. It was below 100 degrees. This was it. Go time.

"Dad, Grandpa, her temperature is below 100 degrees!"

"Call me if you want me to help," his father said, "I'd like to watch."

"City folk," Grandpa commented. "Let nature take its course. You should watch a draft horse foal get born. Now there's something. Everything's gonna be alright. I'll see you in the morning. Don't wake me."

All the lights were off except the kerosene lantern set low on the kitchen table. Josh lay on his sleeping bag with a flashlight and studied over and over the veterinarian's information, all the while keeping an eye on Peach. He propped his head up with the palm of his hand so he would stay awake, but his eyes kept trying to close. He slapped himself gently and quietly hummed some of his favorite tunes to fight off sleep. Finally, he could no longer resist. He dozed off.

He woke up with a start! What was that whining? Where was he? As he got his bearings he realized it was getting light outside. He'd slept the whole night. Startled, he jumped up and looked at Peach. She was lying comfortably on her side nursing six little newborn puppies, looking calm and proud as a new mama. There was hardly any sign of the sacs. He felt only dampness on her blankets.

"Dad, Grandpa, hurry," he shouted. His dad and Grandpa ran quickly to him half asleep in their underwear.

"The new pups have arrived," Noah almost shouted. "Great work, Josh."

"Well, actually, you'd better say 'Great work, Peach' since I didn't have to do a thing," he said bowing his head with embarrassment. "I fell asleep and when I woke up it was all over."

"Told ya," said Grandpa with a wink.

15
OPEN WATER

"I've got a great idea," Noah said to Josh one morning in late spring. "Let's take Grandpa's boat for a trip to North Manitou Island. It's a beautiful little sanctuary, far enough away from the mainland that most people never visit it. I used to go there when I was working on the fishing boats. But that's another story."

"I know," Josh said with a bit of a smile. "Sounds like a good trip."

They made plans to leave in two days. On the day of the trip, a morning rain shower passed to the east, unveiling blue sky. The rising sun began to heat the morning coolness. Grandpa was his high-spirited self and had gotten up before dawn to get breakfast going. Noah had gotten up early, too. He had already been out to the boat to check the engine, steering, and boat trailer for their trip to North Manitou Island.

Josh sat up in bed, listening to the familiar and reassuring sounds of creaking floorboards and clanging iron pans. Absent this morning was the familiar sound of his wind-up alarm clock. Grandpa had borrowed it to put under the bedding of the puppies that Peach had had nearly four weeks before. The puppies were being weaned from Peach, which meant they'd have to learn to eat on their own and not depend on their mother for her milk. They were separated from her now in their own crib next to Peach's bed. His grandfather said when puppies first get separated from their mother, the ticking sound of the clock comforted them and reminded them of their mother's heartbeat.

Josh had not decided which puppy he would choose, but was excited it would be his very own to care for.

He got out of bed and walked over to the rail. The smell of wood smoke sharpened the air as he idly contemplated the wisps of smoke curling and rising, then flattening against the ceiling. Josh looked down at his father and grandfather cooking breakfast.

Grandpa Oggy's beard was shorter. About a month before, Noah said he was sick of looking at Grandpa Oggy's unkempt beard. It was not only scraggly but had served as a bib that caught the maple syrup that inevitably dripped down when he ate breakfast. They had sat him down in the middle of the barnyard where Noah proceeded to trim Grandpa's beard, dropping mounds of white hair onto the ground. Later they would discover some of the white beard woven into a robin's nest at the edge of the woods.

As Josh climbed down the ladder, Peach stood up from her bed and wagged her tail to greet him, just as she did every morning. The puppies began to whine when they saw Peach move. Josh knew the puppies wanted their mother.

During breakfast Grandpa Oggy said, "Now that we have enough logs and lumber we can finish the two-bedroom addition for you two before the black flies get thick. If we work hard we should be done in a month or so. You're gonna learn some good carpenter skills, Josh."

"Should be interesting," Josh said. He had worked through the winter pulling logs out of the forest with Grandpa. They had milled the round logs for the outside of the cabin, and had cut other logs into boards to make roof rafters.

Josh had been fascinated to see the math he had learned in his schoolbooks put to practical use as Grandpa assembled the first rafters. Using a carpenter square, Grandpa could triangulate various geometrical angles Josh was familiar with to cut the ends of the rafters. Josh had also figured out why Grandpa kept his fingernails so long after trying to pick up the carpenter square himself. It was easier with longer fingernails.

Josh had learned by listening and watching. He had followed and mimicked Grandpa's every move. Grandpa Oggy had given him a nail pouch to wear around his waist. He'd even worn a cap with a flat carpenter's pencil sticking out the side and had learned how to spit like Grandpa Oggy without his saliva running down his chin. Noah had tried to help with the logs and rafters as much as he could, but he was usually too busy going to the feed store or grocery shopping or cleaning the cabin or sitting at his laptop making a living. But Josh understood. He knew his father was performing tasks his mother once did, and more.

Josh and Noah watched Grandpa Oggy eat his breakfast. The maple syrup was building up on the front of his bib overalls, which meant it was time again to talk Grandpa into changing his clothes so they could wash them.

"Dad," Noah said, "I'm running a load of wash this afternoon after we get back from our trip out to North Manitou, so take those bibs off so we can get them in the wash."

Grandpa kept eating.

"Dad," Noah repeated, "will you please change while we're gone so I can throw them in the wash this afternoon?"

Gripping his spoon sideways, not looking up from his bowl, Grandpa Oggy answered, "You know, when my beard was longer this didn't happen."

After breakfast the three of them walked out to the boat, walking with the same synchronized gait—single file, from oldest to youngest, in what seemed to be a choreographed father-son dance. Josh and Noah piled into the truck and Grandpa waved goodbye as they headed down the two-track to launch their boat at Good Harbor Bay.

When they reached the bay, they unhitched the boat, slid it off the trailer, and skidded it across the sand to the lake.

Josh whispered as his father stared out over the open water. "Dad, I've never seen the bay so still and flat. You can't hear anything. It's so quiet."

"It sure is," Noah said. "I hate to disrupt the silence to start the boat motor. But if we're going to get to North Manitou Island, I guess I have to."

They climbed in the boat, and Noah used an oar to push it into deeper water so he could lower the motor. The boat motor coughed to life when Noah pushed the starter button, and the two of them headed out into Lake Michigan for their trip to the island.

16
NORTH MANITOU ISLAND

~~~~~~

Their boat was an eighteen-foot wooden boat his father and grandfather had built years before Josh was born. It was constructed with overlapping shiplap boards of reddish-brown mahogany. Its hull was heavy and deep. His grandfather had installed a steering wheel connected by cables to the stern, or rear of the boat, and the rebuilt forty-horsepower outboard motor.

Noah had bought a camera soon after they moved north and said he was eager to take up wildlife photography. This trip would give him a chance to photograph a small Caspian tern colony he had heard about that lived along the coast near Donner Point. The island is some ten miles from shore—an island wilderness protected by water. Unlike the mainland, North Manitou Island's wild creatures have little human contact. Due to their lack of fear, Noah could take closer, dramatic portraits of the fledgling birds.

This morning they skimmed across a bay so flat that it reflected like an azure-blue mirror. The North and South Manitou Islands loomed on the horizon.

"You know, Josh, the Ojibwa Indians thought those two islands were lost bear cubs," Noah said over the hum of the engine.

"No kidding."

"They believed that a mother bear and her two cubs fled a Wisconsin forest fire by attempting to swim to Michigan. The mother made it, her cubs did not. She waited on the sandy shore for her cubs and became what is today called the Sleeping Bear Dunes. The Great Spirit took pity on her and raised her cubs up from the depths, forming North and South Manitou Islands."

"Wow, I can kinda see that now when I look at the islands."

Thirty minutes later the silence returned to drift-still as Noah cut the motor and they slid onto the island's shore sand. Josh stared hypnotically at the boat's water trail as it disappeared into the calmness of the lake. As they climbed out of the boat, Caspian terns took to the air, orbiting and noisily crying out their shrill objections at the two intruders. But the terns did not go far; they had youngsters to care for.

Within a short time the terns—largely white birds with black caps and bright red bills—slowly circled down and returned to their young, their cries now reduced to occasional low, hoarse *kowk* sounds. Some terns watched inquisitively, first standing on one leg and then the other, as the intruders unloaded their gear from the boat. Others preened the feathers of their chicks, and the chicks sounded their contentment with high-pitched whistles.

The spring air had a cool edge to it, especially after the brisk trip across the lake. Josh sat back on the sandy beach and warmed his bones in the radiant heat of the sun. He looked forward to putting to use lessons Grandpa had taught him last winter about how to look for animals in the wild. With Grandpa he had practiced being part of the environment. He learned to walk slower, sometimes stopping, narrowing his vision to look for individual shapes or slight movements and sounds. He would stand still for long periods, turning his head slowly—looking, smelling, listening. One time he had spotted a coyote peering back at him, for how long he did not know. It had been disguised within the camouflage of the forest like a piece of a jigsaw puzzle.

This morning he walked slowly through beach grass and then squatted within a nonthreatening distance of a mother tern and her babies. Noah had a high-powered telescopic lens on his camera, which let him set up far enough away so as not to disturb the birds but still get a good close-up. He quickly snapped a picture of Josh with the terns, then another when Josh turned and smiled.

"Perfect, Josh," his father said, "but not too close. We don't want to disturb the chicks."

Josh backed away as slowly as he had approached the birds and stood only when he thought the birds would be at ease.

Josh watched as his father took photos. He watched his father's body language—his arm and leg movements, his expressions. He watched as his father set up his camera and tripod, peered through the camera lens with a tight-lipped smile, and gave a slight sigh of self-contentment after he squeezed his finger on the camera's shutter release.

As the morning deepened toward noon, Josh and Noah started back to the boat so they could eat the lunch they had packed and then return home. His father had to stop more often on the return walk to switch his camera gear from one shoulder to the other, the pace of his strides now slowing. As they retraced their steps, the energetic early morning footprints they now observed upside-down were spaced farther apart. Next to the larger footprints were Josh's smaller set, which would suddenly leap out of line and run circles around the larger prints, or make short forays, sometimes leading to the water's edge or up into the woods. Now, tired, Josh and his father both walked through the beach sand in a straight line.

For Josh, the most interesting observation of the morning was of a piping plover that looked hurt—one wing drooped awkwardly and appeared broken.

"Look, Dad, that bird is hurt."

"Not really, Josh. It's trying to fake us out. It wants to lead us away from its young chicks."

Josh backtracked to where he had first seen the mother plover. Sure enough, there was the flock of chicks, lying flat against the sand in a cluster of dune grass.

His father also explained that these birds were endangered and that this was one of the few places in the world where they nested. They cut a wide circle around the birds to avoid bothering the young.

They had beached the boat near a barkless, water-worn log that was bleached nearly pure white from the sun. They had stashed the cooler with their lunch in it on the shady side of the log. Now they grabbed the cooler, straddled the log, and laid out their lunch between them.

Josh looked out at the huge lake. "You know, Dad, last week when I was walking the beach I met some tourists staring out at the lake. I think they were from the East Coast somewhere. One of 'em said it looked like the ocean, and then bent over and took a handful of lake water and tasted it. He said he expected it to be salty, like Lake Michigan was one of the oceans."

"Lake Michigan does have a sea-like presence, doesn't it?" his father said.

Josh and his father chatted about their morning experiences and then settled into silence. The only sound heard between the crunching sound of sandwich wrappers opening and closing was the rhythmic sound of wavelets lapping the shoreline.

In about a half hour they finished their sandwiches. They were made with the soft store-bought bread that Josh liked much more than the homemade bread that Grandpa baked. Both sat quietly on the log, sharing sips of sweet clover honey tea from a thermos. While Josh stirred sand with a piece of driftwood, Noah's eyes focused to the north, where the horizon met the water.

As they finished their tea, a strong breeze picked up out of the northwest. Noah perked up and turned his face toward the lake. The water was coming alive, gradually forming slight rolls. The quiet early morning water was beginning to create sounds.

Josh noticed his dad's expression. "What are you looking at, Dad?"

"Oh, nothing I guess. The water's picking up and I'm looking at the clouds." The clear blue sky was beginning to fill with big puffy clouds.

"What do you see in the clouds?"

"You see those darker clouds mixed in with the white ones over there coming toward us? Just might be a storm coming our way."

Josh watched his father reach over and grab his pack, quickly open it, then nervously rummage through his gear. "Hey Josh, do you remember seeing the cell phone? Is it in your backpack?"

"No, I didn't take it. I saw it this morning on the counter in the charger. You're the only one who uses it."

"How stupid can I be," Noah said. "We better head for Good Harbor if we're going to beat the weather."

Josh stood up quickly and felt a little shiver of fear.

"Don't worry, Josh," Noah added. "Let's just get loaded up."

Josh looked out over the water, noticing whitecaps brewing about a mile offshore. It looked like it would be a bumpy ride.

"We need to launch now, and I mean now," his father said with more urgency than before.

They threw their gear into the boat, pushed the boat off the beach, and were not at full throttle before the water changed from a chop to whitecaps that pounded the boat. Josh was always required to wear his life vest in the boat, but he felt another wave of fear sweep over him as he watched his father don a life vest for the first time.

"Zip your vest, Dad," Josh yelled to his father. "You always tell me to zip mine."

"I can't. It's too small," his father yelled back.

The weather was getting serious—the water crashing against the boat's hull soon muffled the sound of the outboard motor. The temperature began to drop and the breeze grew into heavy winds that drove the waves from the west. Josh's father needed to steer southeast to get to shore but he had to cut across the waves at an angle to avoid capsizing the boat. There was no turning back now.

"Lie belly down and hold on to something!" his father yelled.

Josh dropped to the bottom of the boat. Sheets of cold water began to spray over the sides and pummel his back, making his body twitch. He screamed in shock.

"Don't worry, Josh. Everything's gonna be all right. Just hang on!"

Time after time, mile after mile, Josh could hear the

boat motor's muffled whine as his father throttled up a wave, and he felt the wooden planks shudder as the boat surfed down and crashed into the bottom of a swell. The water in the boat was getting so deep Josh had to keep his head raised to breathe. His neck began to hurt from trying to keep his head up. He knelt on all fours and looked over the bow. Just then the boat was rocked by a wave and he lost his balance, banging his head on the inside of the boat.

"Stay down, Josh!"

He went back down, straining to keep his head above water. A trickle of blood ran down his forehead. He noticed the water in the boat turning red.

They had reached the outer edge of Good Harbor Bay when the most massive wave of the day slammed the side of the boat and sent Josh flying. In a second he was submerged in cold, bubbling water. When Josh bobbed up to the surface, the world was a blur and the boat was nowhere in sight. Did the boat capsize? Did his father get thrown from boat? Adrenaline rushed through his blood and he could feel his heart drumming in his ears. Arms and legs flailing, he swam frantically, trying to stay above water. Was this a nightmare? Or was he living the nightmare?

Josh screamed for his father, but the howling wind drowned him out. He saw only water and sky in perpetual motion—wild sea-like waves that sent him violently up and down the peaks and valleys, and swirling purple storm clouds that lit the sky over his head with lightning bolts followed by explosions of ear-piercing thunder.

He tried to swim but had no idea of which direction to head. The added weight of his soaked clothing and shoes drew him deeper into the lake in spite of his life vest, and he fought to keep his mouth above the waterline. The minutes seemed like hours as the waves sucked him beneath the water, cutting off his breath. He instinctively pushed upwards with his arms to inhale a few more precious puffs of air before he was sucked under again. Josh's fingers began to stiffen, his ears numbed, and every muscle in his body tightened down to his toes.

Josh coughed up water and cried out for his father, but his voice was weak and broken against the keening wind. His teeth chattered uncontrollably, his head ached like it never had before, and his stomach cramped. He vomited a bellyful of cold water. Josh tried to scream again for his father, but his voice was now reduced to a feeble groan. He couldn't fight the cold waves and wind any longer. He knew he was beginning to drown.

Just as he felt his head might sink beneath the waves for the last time, Josh thought he heard a wind-disguised voice leak from between waves. He didn't want to lift his head to look, thinking it was his imagination—but he did. And there, riding the surf, was their boat. It was his father heading directly at him. As the boat skirted past him, Josh

felt a tug on the back of his life vest. Suddenly he was flying out of the water and he came crashing down on the
floorboards of the boat. He looked up to see his father, his
face taut with tension.

"You all right?" Noah shouted. "It took me a long time
to turn around!" Josh noticed him wince and heard his
father's trembling voice, "Thank God I found you. We
gotta get this thing to shore." But Josh just lay limp with
his head propped up against the front of the boat, too
exhausted to respond.

As the motor whined and struggled with every wave,
Josh heard his father yell that he saw treetops, and then
heard him scream, "Whaleback Bluff!" over the sound of
the storm. It was then he knew they were close to shore.

Out of nowhere Josh was startled by the rapid *thump*,
thump, *thump* of something directly over his head. Seconds
later a Coast Guard rescue helicopter appeared out of the
mist, hovering above the two of them. The force of the
whirling blades felt like a storm within the storm, flattening the waves around them in a large circle. Within
minutes his father had maneuvered the boat to the
shallows, and the boat pitched up on the beach like a
piece of driftwood.

Noah grabbed the boat's bow rope and pulled the boat
farther up on the sand, and lifted Josh out of the boat. They
both collapsed on the beach.

"By God you made it," they heard out of the mist. Grandpa Oggy emerged in his yellow rain slicker, directed his face upwards, and waved both his arms in the air to signal the helicopter that everything was under control, but the rescue chopper stayed and hovered over them. Grandpa took off his slicker and covered Josh with it.

"I was watching you fellas through my binoculars from the bluff and glassed Josh go overboard. I hightailed it back to the cabin and called 911 and they said they was gonna call the Coast Guard. Anyways, I guess it didn't turn out to be the right day to go to North Manitou did it? You guys scared the daylights out of me. Say Josh, what's that blood on your head?"

Josh poked his trembling arm out from beneath the slicker and wiped his hand across his face and saw blood on his palm. Still trying to recover, he looked up at Grandpa Oggy and attempted to answer, but was just too cold and tired to reply. Then the three of them heard the yelp of sirens, a moment later Deputy Bartelli and rescue medics emerged from the woods. The Coast Guard helicopter then banked, gained altitude, and in a moment was gone.

17
THE SECOND WINTER

Josh walked from the cabin to the barn. He slid open the barn doors. Babe and Anna, Grandpa Oggy's two black Percheron draft horses, turned their heads and neighed. It was cold, and steam blew out of their nostrils and rose from their backs. They rubbed their heads against the stall boards enthusiastically, anticipating a trip to the woods. Each was heavy and tall—over seventeen hands high. "Hands" was how they measured horses, Grandpa said. Seventeen hands was just under six feet high at the withers—the place where the horse's shoulders meet its neck. Each weighed over two thousand pounds—more than a ton of muscled horseflesh. Together Babe and Anna represented two tons of living, pulling horsepower.

"Hi Babe, hi Anna. Are you ready to go out and play?"

It was logging day.

He removed Babe and Anna from their stalls one at a time and tied them off, side by side, in the center of the barn. When he had first moved to the cabin, he had been frightened to death of these huge animals. Grandpa had slowly taught him how to handle the horses until the fear went away. Josh soon realized they were gentle creatures.

He had confidence handling them now, and they could sense it. Josh could rig them almost as fast as Grandpa Oggy did, but what slowed him down was the fact that, at age thirteen, he was still too short to harness them without using a stepladder. Just the weight of the draft horse harnesses, or riggings as Grandpa called them, was more than Josh weighed. But Josh was proud that a kid his size could handle two tons of horses with relative ease now.

He went into the tack room to gather the equipment. On the walls hung various leather riggings dating back many years. Off in a corner was a leather-mending table.

Josh paused for a moment, remembering how cunning Grandpa Oggy was. That first winter Grandpa had hitched a toboggan behind the horses and taught Josh to ride on it standing up. The trick Grandpa Oggy played on him was that he actually was teaching Josh how to log surf, which meant that as you were driving the team of horses you jumped on top of the log and rode it. It was faster than slowly walking alongside the log as the horses pulled it. And it was a thrill to see how fast you could go without falling off. Grandpa Oggy said log surfing was for young men—he was too old to surf the logs himself any more.

Josh leaned against the mending table, rubbing his calloused hands to keep them warm, and looked at photographs Grandpa Oggy had nailed to the wall. He saw a picture of his mother holding him when he was a baby. He smiled. There was also a Christmas card with a photo of his mother, father, and himself. They were all dressed up and smiling. The professional photographer had surrounded them with red poinsettias for a holiday family portrait.

"Classy picture," he thought to himself. Life back in Birmingham had been more sophisticated, more refined. "City folk," Grandpa would call them.

During this second winter in the North Country, Birmingham was beginning to fade from Josh's memory. He was beginning to enjoy the country life. Now he felt as comfortable in Carhartt jeans and a flannel shirt as he once did in his designer-label clothes. He was going native like his dad.

Josh took the horse brush off the mending table and walked back to Babe and Anna. He brushed them both thoroughly, especially around their shoulders where the collar rests. When he was done, he went back to the tack room, gathered the harness equipment, and laid it down in front of the horses. He put his stepladder in front of the horses and, one at a time, placed the collar over the horse's

head. Next he put on the hames and back pad, and then the britchen. He hooked the hames around the collar and fastened the hames strap, along with the trace, backstrap, and hip assembly. He then went to the rear and pulled the britchen over the horse's rump.

He always was very careful around the horses. They were so big that they could crush his foot just by stepping on it. One bump from the side would send a grown man flying down hard to the ground.

Josh went around the front of the horses and climbed his ladder, put the bit in each horse's mouth, and gently

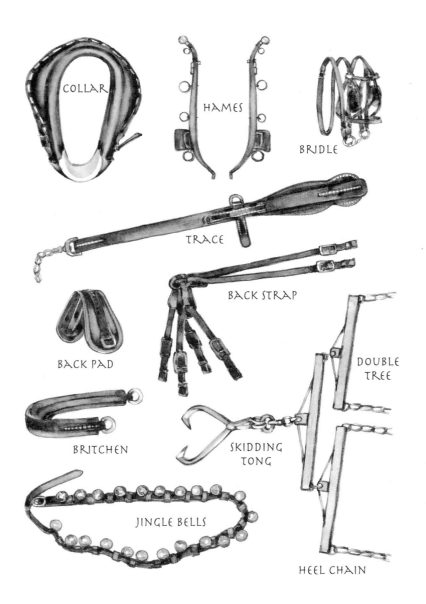

COLLAR

HAMES

BRIDLE

TRACE

BACK STRAP

BACK PAD

DOUBLE TREE

BRITCHEN

SKIDDING TONG

JINGLE BELLS

HEEL CHAIN

pulled the bridle over the head and ears. Finally he hooked up the twenty-foot reins to each horse.

He took the reins in his hand and gently said, "Back easy." Babe and Anna walked backwards until he said, "Whoa."

Babe ate enormous amounts of hay and always had gas. He let out gas that sounded like someone letting air out of a big balloon. The sound and the smell of this used to make Josh gag, but now he only said, "Aw, Babe, that wasn't very polite." The horses could amuse him, too. The first time he saw Anna burp—she had opened her mouth, tilted her head up, curled her lips, showed her teeth like she was laughing, and let out a belch—he almost fell to the ground because he was laughing so hard.

He bent over and connected the doubletree to the heel chain and hooked on the skidding tong.

He then said to the horses, "Step up," and made a kissing sound with his lips. The giant pair went forward out of the barn. Immediately Josh followed up with the command "Gee," the signal for turning right. They turned and he stopped them outside in front of the barn. Then he remembered that he wanted to put on the "jingle bells," so he returned to the barn. He liked to hear the bells when the horses walked.

While he was wrapping the bells around Babe and Anna, his father came out of the cabin and said, "You can help Grandpa until about two o'clock, but then you gotta come inside and study. I'm going to Traverse City today."

"Can't I just do the studying tomorrow?" Josh begged.

"You said that yesterday. You don't want to get behind, do you? I think you'd better do it today, Josh."

"But I'm not behind. I'm ahead."

His father tilted his head in the familiar gesture that said there was no hope of changing his mind today.

"Okay, Dad," Josh reluctantly said. Schoolwork had always been easy, still was, and he liked learning. But it got in the way of working with Grandpa Oggy in the woods. Besides, Grandpa loved to tell stories, and Josh loved to listen to them.

18
LOG SURFING

Before Josh took the horses into the woods with Grandpa Oggy, his dad asked him if he would go down to the road to get the newspaper and see if the county snowplow had gone by yet. By now a trip to the mailbox or to get the paper was routine, and Josh hopped into the old Chevy Apache.

"Wait a minute," his dad said, "I'll go with you. Do you mind if I drive? I haven't driven that critter in a long time."

"Sure," Josh answered. "You remember how?"

"Very funny."

His dad pulled out the manual choke and timer, pushed in the clutch, gave it some gas, and turned the key. The old truck sputtered to a start like it always did. He pushed the choke and timer in, grabbed the shift and put it down into first gear, let out the clutch, gave it some gas, and they were on their way.

Noah turned on the windshield wipers to push away the snow. The wipers flapped erratically, one going up as the other went down. Grandpa Oggy was probably the only man left in the county who didn't have four-wheel drive. Instead, he always put tire chains on the rear wheels, which made a rattling sound when the tires rotated.

"You know, I hate Grandpa driving this truck," Noah said. "It's dangerous, and I'm not sure that driving with chains isn't against the law. I doubt that he's even renewed his driver's license in years. Grandpa was so proud when he bought this Chevy."

About halfway to the main road his father asked Josh, "You remember last summer when we drove by Grandpa walking down the side of the road picking up bottles and cans?

"Yeah, I've seen lots of people do that, mainly bums, I guess."

"I know. It used to embarrass me when I saw him picking up bottles as I rode by in the school bus. He was quite the bottle gatherer. My friends thought he was an oddball. Maybe some people still think he's scraping for a dollar because he's so poor. Truth is, he probably has more money in the bank than a majority of the people living around here. He's just frugal—to the extreme."

Noah slowed the truck to a stop. "Here we are. The main road looks plowed."

"Yep, I'll get the newspaper and check the mailbox," Josh said.

Back at the cabin, his dad shut off the truck. Then, as an afterthought, he added, "When I was in high school I used to tell Grandpa he should sell all this land. He'd be a millionaire, you know."

"What'd he say?"

"The answer was always the same: 'So once I got the million dollars, then what am I gonna do?'"

Josh shook his head. "Sounds like Grandpa, all right." He climbed out of the truck.

"Don't tell him what I told you just now, okay? I'll see you later."

"Okay, Dad. Drive careful."

Grandpa and the horses were waiting. "You ready to go, Josh? I'll steer Babe and Anna up to the timber cut and then we'll tong 'em and you can surf 'em back down here."

"Ready? I'm always ready for this. Let's head up to the woods."

Grandpa turned to Babe and Anna, made a kissing sound with his lips, and said, "Step up." The horses moved forward, Josh swung the cant hook up onto his shoulder, and they headed up to the timber.

When they reached the spot where the trees had recently been felled, Grandpa Oggy shouted "Haw," the signal for Babe and Anna to turn left into the woods. He steered them with the reins to the first log and shouted, "Gee, Anna, Gee Babe," and the horses turned right. Grandpa then said "Whoa" when they came up to the side of the first log. Both horses stopped just as they had been trained to do.

They walked in silence to the front of the fallen log. Josh listened to the forest talk. The new snow created a hush in the woods. He could hear the lyrics of snowbirds, red squirrels chattering, and the occasional sharp report of woodpeckers' beaks tapping on the trees.

"Bring the cant hook," Grandpa said.

Josh handed him the long pole with a movable metal hook at one end. Grandpa rolled the log with the cant hook and fastened the tongs to the front of the first log. Then he took the reins. "Step up," he commanded, and the horses began to pull the log to the trail. When the huge log was straight on the logging trail, he stopped the horses and handed the reins to Josh. "Okay, surf 'er down."

Josh stood to the side of Babe and Anna, made the kissing sound, and said "Step up. Barn." The horses knew what "barn" meant and didn't need any other direction as they began to pull the log. Josh walked alongside the log as the horses pulled. Then he loosened the reins just a bit, the horses picked up speed, and he jumped onto the log and began his surf ride. He couldn't think of anything more exciting than surfing logs—except that for sure and for certain when he was a little older and stronger he wanted to kiteboard the waves in the lake like the bigger kids did. In the summer he'd sat on the beach and watched the kiteboarders' chutes lift them off the surf into the air, and heard their screams of excitement. Nothing was going to hold him back from doing that.

"I'll get the next log ready," Grandpa yelled. "See you when you get back."

Josh tried to keep his balance on the log all the way back without falling off, and only once or twice did he have to step off the log and then jump back on.

He returned with the horses to see Grandpa Oggy smiling, leaning against the cant hook pole. When Josh stopped Babe and Anna next to the log that was going to be surfed his Grandpa said, "Remember when I told you your Dad's nickname in school was 'Smokey'?"

"Yeah," Josh said, wiping his runny nose with his coat sleeve after he noticed Grandpa Oggy's nose running, the watery liquid trickling down onto his beard and freezing.

"Well, I never told you why. In the wintertime when he was in middle school, I noticed that he started to hang his school clothes outside on the front porch at night before he went up to bed. Then he'd go out in the cold in the mornin' in his underwear and put on his clothes that were outside all night. And without comin' back in the cabin, he would walk down to the end of the two-track to meet the school bus. But I didn't pay too much attention to why he was doin' all this. Then one day I spotted his red-checked wool mackinaw coat hanging from a tree limb in the woods when I went out to get the mail. I went out to the tree limb and took the coat back to the cabin. That afternoon yer pa came runnin' up from the two-track freezin' and the front door flew open when he came bargin' in.'"

Josh put down the reins and sat on a tree stump. This was going to be good. Another story.

"Anyways," Grandpa Oggy said, "yer pa saw the coat hangin' on the back of a kitchen chair, and I asked what his coat was doin' hangin' on the tree limb. I learned a lot after this, and it wasn't pretty. He was just about froze to death and got mad at me. We'd had a heavy snow that afternoon and yer pa thought the coat had fell off the tree limb and got buried. I guess he clawed the snow with his bare hands for a long while searchin' for his coat, then gave up."

"He must not have liked his coat," said Josh.

"Yep, but there's more to it. Now comes the 'Smokey' nickname. What I found out was he was embarrassed that the coat made him look like a lumberjack. He didn't like that. And the reason he hung his clothes outside was because he didn't want to smell like wood smoke, so he aired 'em out all night. I always liked the smoke smell. But to him it was embarrassin'. The kids used to think that folks who smelled like wood smoke were poor, because they couldn't afford a regular furnace like the one you used to have at your old house down in Birmingham. So, that's how he got the name 'Smokey.' His classmates gave it to 'im. He had a hard time with it. To me, it was just how we were. I didn't know. We got into a pretty good scrap about it. Kinda like the one we had when you were mad about the baby-fat blisters on yer hands."

"Yeah, I get it," Josh responded. "Back downstate at school we made fun of kids, too. We were always comparing clothes, houses, swimming pools, who had the most expensive cell phones and who didn't, the kind of car your parents drove. That kind of stuff."

"Your pa might have thought we were poor, but I never did and still don't compared to how I grew up."

"What do you mean?"

"My family migrated up north with my grandfather, your great-great-grandfather. He was a sawyer from Arkansas who followed the lumberjacks when they cut the great virgin pines that used to grow here. My pa was born here when the big-time loggin' was over. All the big virgin white pines were cut down. He ended up cuttin' and splittin' firewood for other folks to scrape a livin'.

"When I come along it was the Great Depression. Times were tough and we were dirt poor. I made up my mind when I grew up I was goin' to make something of myself. I'm proud of what I have here. Me and Grandma bought this land together and built all this with our own hands. Every log in that cabin was skidded out of the woods and put up by yer grandma and me with a team of horses. She even swung a hammer with me to build the mill and barn. We did it all by ourselves. I thought we were rich compared to your great-grandparents. But your pa didn't."

"I guess there's a big difference on what the meaning of rich and poor is," Josh commented.

"Anyways," Grandpa continued, as he lifted his arms with the palms of his hands facing up to the sky, "how could it get any better than this?"

"Yeah Grandpa, this is pretty great. And I'm glad you don't call my dad 'Smokey' anymore. He hated that nickname as much as I hated 'Cubby.' "

Grandpa just laughed. "I guess you can teach an old dog new tricks, eh?" Then he pulled his pocket watch out of the top of his bib overalls, flipped open the lid, and said, "Well, I guess you gotta go back and study now like yer pa said."

"I guess so, if I have to," Josh said.

"You don't want me to get into trouble with yer pa do ya?"

They were working within sight of the bluff that overlooked Good Harbor Bay. Grandpa pointed toward the bay and asked, "Hey, before you go back, ya wanna take a walk over to the edge of the bluff?"

"Sure," Josh replied without hesitation.

They did not talk while they walked. Silence breathed between their crunching footsteps, which overlapped at times with the sound of the ravens perched in the treetops . . . *rrronk . . . rrronk . . . rrronk.*

When they reached the edge of the bluff, they looked over its edge. Far below huge chunks of ice piled on each other with a loud thudding sound. Beyond the ice, the waves pushed mounds of slush toward shore. The tremendous force of it all was awesome.

"The lake is moving—freezing, thawing, and refreezing," Grandpa said. "It's always changing." Josh watched the never-ending movement below and remembered the panic he felt when he was plunged into the water the previous spring.

"Hey Grandpa, you remember last summer when we saw that huge freighter going through the Manitou Passage?"

"Yeah, it was quiet that mornin'. Remember how we could hear its big engines chuggin' along when it was so quiet? It was the only sound we could hear. Hard to believe that so many of those huge freighters have gone down in storms. There's a powerful beast hidden inside that lake. I guess you remember that from last spring. Lucky yer pa has experience out there. Yer pa's been caught in the beast back when he worked the fishing boats. But it's mighty pretty when it ain't actin' up."

Josh bent over and packed a snowball and threw it over the side. It seemed forever until the snowball hit the ice.

Grandpa Oggy pulled out his pocket watch and flipped open the cover. "It's almost two-thirty. You really gotta get home before your pa catches us. You cut through the woods; it's shorter."

Josh started trudging through the snow in the direction of the cabin.

"And don't tell yer dad what I told ya today about him," Grandpa Oggy yelled after him.

"I won't," Josh said, a bit breathless as he struggled through the snow.

19
BABE AND ANNA
STAND ALONE

From his desk, Josh peered through the window, unable to buckle down to study. Silver-dollar-size snowflakes fell undisturbed and silent in the windless air, laying a new carpet of white dust in the barnyard. He walked over to the wood stove, opened the door, chucked in a couple of logs, and stood looking at the fire for a moment.

He thought about another story his grandfather had told him. According to Grandpa, Noah had borrowed a diesel log skidder from a neighbor and brought it up into the woods one day when Oggy was in town. He brought it into the woods to show off how much faster the machine could haul logs compared to the horses. Grandpa said the skidder had torn up the woods like a tornado had touched down.

He had acted out the whole scene to Josh—moving his

body and arms, telling the story as if it were yesterday. "I yanked yer pa off the skidder onto his back in the snow and yelled at him, pointin' my finger into his face . . ." Grandpa said, waving one of his big crooked fingers ". . . then I shouted, 'Noah, don't let me catch you and that monster you're drivin' up here ever again!'"

Josh sympathized with his grandfather's "gentle to the forest" principle; he had read articles recently about how people were using horses in the forest more often, calling it "low-impact forest floor logging."

But Josh's real focus was on how Grandpa also said he felt bad about losing his temper at his son. He said after that day Noah had become harder to talk to, more distant and unapproachable. Josh remembered his similar reaction to his own father's stern discipline.

He closed the door of the wood stove and sat back down at his desk. Before long, he dozed off, his head and arms lying on top of his books. He awakened suddenly when he heard a horse whinny outside the window. He looked out and saw it was dusk. Babe and Anna were standing in front of the barn. Grandpa must be back, he thought to himself. He put on his coat and walked out to the barn. "Grandpa?" he called. There was no answer. He yelled "Grandpa" loudly inside the barn. Still no response. He went outside and yelled for his grandpa in all directions into the woods. No answer.

He walked over to the horses and then behind them. Four inches of new snow had fallen. He saw the horses' tracks leading from the main trail and drag marks from the tong and reins—but no human footprints. Josh began to get frantic. *What if he had a heart attack up on the bluff just after I left him?* "What happened?" he said aloud to Babe and Anna. He paced beside the horses trying to think of what to do. He wished his dad was home.

Finally, he decided to take the horses up the trail to find Grandpa. He picked up the reins but then dropped them. *How would he get him back here?* He ran into the barn looking for something to carry Grandpa on.

On the wall, he spotted the perfect answer—the toboggan. He took it down and ran back to the horses with it, attaching it behind them. He kept shouting "Haw!" until they turned completely around. He took a good hold on the reins and yelled "Step up!" and they began to walk. He loosened the reins and yelled "Yah!" and they broke into a gallop. He ran alongside the toboggan and then jumped on, stood with his knees bent, and loosened the reins all the way. He was going as fast as he ever had. Fast enough to hear the wind blowing in his ears.

He galloped the horses up to where they had worked earlier and stopped them. "Grandpa," he yelled once, and then again. At the second yell he heard a faint, "Over here. Over here, Josh."

The sound came from a side trail, and Josh turned the horses and sent them into a gallop again. A few hundred feet up the side trail he saw Grandpa lying in the snow and waving his arms. He was on his back, almost completely covered with snow. His face was red and his beard frozen with ice. Both his legs were trapped under a log.

"Grandpa!" Josh screamed. "Are you okay?"

"I'm in a bad way," his grandfather replied. "I can't move my legs. They're numb from layin' here so long, I guess."

"I'll get you out," Josh said anxiously.

He ran back to the horses and unhooked the toboggan. He steered the horses to the opposite side of where Grandpa Oggy lay. He hooked up the tongs to the middle of the log and told his grandfather, "I'll go slow. Tell me if you want me to stop if it hurts."

"Go ahead Josh. I'll tell ya if it hurts."

"Step up easy," Josh whispered, and the horses responded. The log began to move slowly off Grandpa's legs. "Everything okay, Grandpa?"

"Yep, keep 'er goin' Josh," Grandpa answered weakly. Josh couldn't help but notice the tortured expression on his face.

When the log was completely off of his grandfather, Josh ran back and got the toboggan and hooked it up behind the horses. He moved Babe and Anna to position the toboggan next to his grandfather and rolled him onto it.

"Okay, here we go, Grandpa."

"Easy on the horses, boy. They're winded."

Josh ignored Grandpa's remark, straddled his body, and wedged his feet between Grandpa Oggy and the edges of the toboggan. "What happened, Grandpa? This kind of stuff doesn't happen to you," he said.

"I thought I'd try to surf a log."

"Grandpa you're not a kid anymore," Josh said shaking his head. "Step up, barn," he shouted and Babe and Anna started for home.

As they went around the last curve, Josh saw headlights at the cabin. His father was standing next to his truck. Josh drove Babe and Anna right up to the front door of the cabin.

"What's going on? What happened to Grandpa?"

"Grandpa fell and got pinned. I think he's hurt."

Josh and his dad carried Grandpa Oggy inside and settled him on the sofa. They checked Grandpa over top to bottom. Nothing was broken as far as they could tell but one knee was red and very swollen. The only pain Grandpa said he felt was a tingle in his legs. They decided that was from his blood circulation being cut off by the log. They stoked up the wood stove and after a while Grandpa said his legs felt much better.

"It's a miracle, but you seem in remarkably good shape," Noah said to Grandpa. "But I think we better have you checked out at the hospital tomorrow, just in case."

"Nonsense," Grandpa responded. "I been through worse than that and never seen a doc."

Josh's dad pulled a pot of soup out of the refrigerator. It was Grandpa's self-proclaimed "world-famous garden soup," which he had made for dinner the day before. The soup was made from winter vegetables his grandfather stored in the root cellar along with morel mushrooms and wild leeks that Josh and his grandfather had picked in the forest the previous spring and stored in the freezer.

Once they were sure Grandpa was resting comfortably, Josh and his father sat down at the kitchen table. The comforting warmth of the wood stove made Josh feel sandy-eyed, his body heavy and relaxed. When the soup was hot enough to eat, Josh served his Grandpa at the sofa. Grandpa sat up and ate heartily. Josh and his dad ate at the kitchen table. When Grandpa was done he hunched down under the covers.

"Boy, that snow sucks the heat out of ya. This is sure a three-dog night," he said.

"Three Dog Night—that's the name of an old rock group, Dad," Noah commented.

"It might be the name of one of yer rock whatevers, but when I was a kid and we were as cold as this, we wanted three dogs in bed with us to keep us warm."

"Three dogs or not," Noah said, "you were sure lucky out there today, Dad."

"Yes, yes, I suppose I was. I was lucky that the tongs came loose so I could send the horses back to the barn. You couldn't send a diesel log skidder back to the barn," he added.

Noah couldn't resist replying, "If you would let me widen and plow those logging trails we could have driven up there."

"Snowmobiles would work," Josh chimed in. "Maybe we should get a snowmobile, Grandpa Oggy!"

"That's just what you guys would want. There'll never be any of those whining snowmobiles up there while I'm alive," Grandpa said. "I can hardly stand using those noisy chainsaws to cut down the trees."

Grandpa stopped and thought for a moment. "Well, I'm just lucky Josh was there to save my life. You did a fine job, young man—as good as any grown man could have. If you hadn't found me, somebody would have found me later froze solid as a rock."

Josh was quiet as they soaked in the warmth of the wood stove. Flickers from the kerosene lamp Oggy kept on the kitchen table reflected across the walls. The steady, low whistle of the teakettle simmering on the wood stove was singing them to sleep. Grandpa started to snore. Josh turned to ask his father a question but he, too, had nodded off in his chair.

Josh got up and moved next to the stove where Peach and Josh's new female pup, Mouse, were curled up together. Lying down on the floor, he wrapped his arms around them as his eyelids grew heavy. For a second his mother flashed through his mind. He knew his life would never be the same without her. But then an unexpected glow of belonging here ran through his body. He felt at home, safe and protected in this refuge beside Good Harbor Bay. And he fell instantly asleep.